Care to Chat?...

Online Dating for the Over 50's

A sharp, fast and comical read – raw, poignant yet insightful. Vicky shares her extraordinary online dating experiences with a refreshing and unique honesty.

Victoria McDonald

Library of Congress Control Number:		2014920488
ISBN:	Hardcover	978-1-4990-3313-7
	Softcover	978-1-4990-3312-0
	eBook	978-1-4990-3314-4

Rev. date: 11/22/2014

To order additional copies of this book, contact:
Xlibris
1-800-455-039
www.Xlibris.com.au
Orders@Xlibris.com.au
698888

Care to Chat?...

Foreword

I'm going to write a book.

I reckon everyone else is having a go at it … why not me?

I read a lot of books, some good, some hard to finish, some hard to start, and some that just look damn attractive and or impressive on my coffee table. I have books that line my bookcase stacked neatly and I've read them all. I only keep books in my bookcase that I've actually read.

I've always been pretty good with words, can debate with most on some local issues or on social media, can do a mean crossword, can and have even written words to music over the years. Damn! I'm even pretty great at Scrabble, and friends find it hard to beat me.

So here I am, ready to write this book. I have myself all ready and primed to start. I've cleaned the house, made my coffee, and walked my little dog Bobbie (the best mate around), who's a happy little guy now. You know, when they look up at you after a run, and their eyes are bright and shiny and they are still panting with their tongues hanging out all wet and askew. God, I love dogs!

I've threatened to write this book for months and months. You know how it is, you say it, but you probably have no connection with actually sitting down and writing a book! A book takes ages to write, and it may become exhaustive and redundant in the meantime. Or the incentive and or motivation can wane, but I'm keen as mustard at the moment to make a start.

At this stage, I have no preconceived ideas as to exactly how I'm going to write this book. I've never written a book before. I'm just going to start typing and see what transpires. I have heard or read somewhere that words expressed in writing can have a cleansing effect, even therapeutic, so we'll see how it goes.

If at the end of writing this I think that someone might benefit from or simply enjoy reading these words of mine, I may look into publishing it. Have absolutely no idea, how one goes about this, and remember thinking the same thing years ago; when I wrote some lyrics and music I thought were very good. I put it on the back bench then, as I simply had no idea how to go about it, and the incentive waned, as often happens.

There's just been so many thoughts, conversations, experiences throughout this journey, that I need to put them all down in words. I actually have written notes from all these experiences into a journal, and they are screaming at me to be released.

I feel that if I don't - I may go quite mad. Or madder than I surely am.

Victoria McDonald

Chapter 1

Online dating has been around for years now. A real chance for single, separated, divorced or widowed people to meet up, connect and actually find a partner they are content to spend the rest of their lives with. Or even better actually fall in love, perhaps marry and get on with their lives together.

I have read somewhere recently that one in five relationships start on an online dating site. An amazing statistic really, which goes to show their popularity.

There was a time that the words "online dating" were said as you swiped your hand over your mouth very quickly. In case people thought you were desperate, and this was the last resort left open to you. Thank goodness these days everyone seems to be at it, or they know someone who is happily or unhappily at it. It seems to be very popular and is no longer hidden under the carpet.

Being in my mid-fifties, the chances of actually meeting someone the "old fashioned way", such as at a supermarket, or in a museum or library, in a train or a night club are scarce. Besides, I don't know anyone over fifty who goes to nightclubs anymore. Not that there's anything wrong with nightclubs, but for most people of a similar age to whom I've spoken, it's simply something we don't want to do.

There is of course, an experience called "Speed Dating". I have only tried this once and once is all that it will ever be. Don't get me wrong, it is apparent that many people find this little journey down the road to love, a very successful one. Sadly, for me – it was not to be.

When I finally summoned up the courage to attend a Speed Dating event one night at a local pub, and after imbibing a few wines for some Dutch courage, the few minutes I had with each unsuspecting suitor before the little bell sounded, were taken up with a lot of stutters, umming and ahhing, nervous gulping and tight smiling leaving me like a deer caught in headlights.

I believe you need to have the fortitude and stamina of an ox to do well with this sort of thing. If you are at all sensitive, you will get hurt for sure. Although, I've always prided myself on the old maxim of "having a go", this experience left me feeling very inadequate and quite depressed at the end of it all.

It was as a result of this experience, that I turned to online dating, in the hope that this process might prove to be somewhat more amenable to me, that it might result in finding a compatible partner with whom to share my life.

These next few chapters are simply my own personal experiences with online dating and a chance perhaps to cleanse or rid myself of these crazy, insightful, hysterical, depressing, and often challenging situations I have found myself in many, many times.

Clearly, before I continue any further, it is probably important that I tell you a little about myself.

I'm not going to bore you with every detail, but just the stuff I feel might be pertinent to my story on online dating experiences.

I was born and raised in Melbourne, Australia, of Scottish heritage with a little Irish thrown in. A perfect mix. My fathers' father was a Scot, and Mum's was Irish. Therefore I have a rich Celtic heritage. But, I am incredibly proud to say I am a fifth generation Aussie, with children who are sixth generation, and grandchildren who are seventh generation.

To me, this is quite unique. I'm not sure there are too many people out there who can actually claim fifth generation status. I like it a lot. I'm a very proud Australian and love our flag. Long may it fly.

My parents were what I suppose you could call middle class, although I've never been sure exactly what those words meant. They sure as hell weren't rich, but then we weren't exactly struggling, either, so middle of the range I guess, is where we were in life.

I had a beautiful, warm, sensitive and funny mother. An Aquarian, she was a blue eyed blonde, with a figure to die for. All curvy in the right places. Of course she hated her curves. Even back in the sixties and beyond, I remember Mum often complaining about her hips, thighs and bum. To me she was just beautiful, and although I hated her at times when I was a reckless, wayward and bad tempered teenager, she was probably my best friend. Mum was a competent golfer, and she and Dad had actually met on a golf course years earlier. Sadly my beautiful mum died when I was in my late 20's, and I've never quite got over it.

Mum loved a sherry or three and a cigarette, and she loved her golf. She also adored entertaining and had a wonderful array of golfing buddies who would come and go from our home, leaving a waft of brandy and cigarette smoke behind. Which incidentally, I found really comforting, and still do today. The aroma of a good time had, is in my book, a good thing.

Mum did most of her entertaining when Dad wasn't around. The booze would be very quickly hidden, neighbours and friends would quickly scuttle to hurtle out the back door, and through the back gate as soon as we heard his car coming down the road. Bloody good hearing we all had – so attuned to the old blue Wolseley thumping down our street. Dinner would be served on the dot at 6.30pm every night. Never earlier or later. It was a miracle the way Mum managed to put a delicious home cooked meal down on the table, every night, at this exact time. On the rare occasion that Dad might be later, we would continue to enjoy the beautiful music Mum would be playing on our old record player ranging from Tchaikovsky, Beethoven, Marty Robbins, Peer Gynt, Gilbert and Sullivan, and my favourite then, The Rolling Stones. Mum's array of diverse albums were thrashed to death, much to our enjoyment. She would often be found dancing around in the kitchen, sherry in hand whilst holding one of our spaniel's paws and singing happily to the music, till Dad got home when everything went quiet.

My father, who is now in his eighty seventh year, lives up in Northern NSW, where he and Mum moved when I was seventeen. They wanted me to move up there with them, but I was very quick to dig my heels in on that idea. I was finally free. There was absolutely no way I was going to stay with them for a second longer, so I was permitted to stay in Melbourne, provided I shared a place with my older brother Angus. Being the youngest of three children, and the only girl, Mum and Dad assumed that Angus would keep an eye on me for them, which of course was a far cry from what actually happened. Angus and I hardly saw one another, which was exactly the way we liked it.

Dad was the typical man and master of the house. What he said was gospel and Mum buckled under him every time. He was a very good provider and he worked hard during our younger years, until he'd had enough, threw it all in and semi-retired in his mid-forties to live up north. He ruled the house, while we kids were living there and was a tight lipped, difficult task master most of the time. The only time I would ever see him loosen up was when he'd had a couple of drinks under his belt, and I loved that softer, fun side of him, rare though it was.

He was the sort of bloke, who, when Mum put on a dinner party, would head upstairs at some stage during the evening, get into his pyjamas and dressing gown, and come back downstairs to sit back at the dinner table just to give the guests the hint.

They usually did. He really didn't like people much at all, and to this day, he lives a very isolated and what I consider must be a lonely life. One of his favourite quotes is "the more I see of people, the more I love my dog". You probably get the picture.

Sadly my Mum passed away in her fifty-eighth year, although she'd always lived a pretty healthy and seemingly stress-free life. She had suffered a massive heart attack. Her presence is felt by me every day, and I will always miss her terribly. Sometimes I swear she's standing right next to me.

Dad never re-married after Mum's death, nor came close to any relationship with any other woman. He still says to this day, that "no woman could ever come close to your mother, dear." Mum is so far up on a pedestal, that no other woman would ever stand a chance. What was really sad was that as I became older, I never thought Dad treated Mum very well. She probably could've used a little more of that love he clearly had for her. So I think he kept his love to himself most of the time.

Dad made each and every decision for me, as a kid and growing up. I would never question this as I figured that's just the way it was. I was the princess, his little girl. He kept me very isolated from the harshness of life. I remember, for example, being a young kid travelling in the car with dad, and he'd see some road kill on the road up ahead. He would make every effort possible to make sure I would be looking out the other way as we drove past. Or, if something on the telly came on, that may be upsetting for little me; he'd find an excuse to get me away from the telly, so I didn't have to watch it. There were so many examples of this that I won't go into each and every one here, but you probably get my drift. It all left me very ill-prepared for life in general, when I was finally living out on my own. I knew jack shit. I was 17 years young with the life skills of a 10 year old.

Mum and Dad were decent and very good human beings. We were rarely beaten or anything horrible like that, and they tried very hard to give us the best they could. Mum even went back to work, after years of being a housewife and mother, just so they could afford to keep us in our private schools. It would've saved them thousands of dollars and anguish, if they had simply asked me what I wanted to do. Both of them had been to private schools, so naturally thought their children should enjoy the same privilege. A normal enough situation I suppose, but diabolical for me.

Chapter 2

I attended Melbourne Church Of England Girls Grammar School, a prestigious private all-girls school in trendy South Yarra. As I had absolutely no freedom at home, my time at school was mostly spent out of the school gates, going out into the real world as I saw it at the time. I actually had a job when I was 14, working as a waitress in a cafe in Collins Street for a little Lebanese fella called Eddie. I would be dropped off at the front school gate by Dad at 7.00am, on his way to the Stock Exchange, and long before anybody else turned up to school. I would go and have a ciggie in the loo, and walk straight out the back gates of the school and catch an old green tram into the city.

With a change of clothes in my school bag and, wearing an apron provided by Eddie, I worked twice a week, and begrudgingly attended school the rest of the time. When I think now of the risks I was taking then, and having 2 daughters of my own, I shiver and squirm. Any money I earned (which wasn't much), I would squander on make-up, cigarettes or clothes, which of course were secretly hidden in my bedroom and never saw the light of day. I learnt how to smoke, and how to forge my Mum's signature to explain my absence from school.

My Mother's signature was a piece of cake, and the many absence notes I forged was impressive. My reports were also fiddled with and I learnt how to forge the headmistresses' signature which was more difficult. However, I practiced and persevered till it was near perfect.

It was very easy to change a C – to a C+ on my reports. A damn good thing when a C- was a fail.

My freedom was thwarted, when finally some bright spark in the school's administration, called Mum at home one afternoon, to ask about my obvious poor health. My many days of absence, although I tried hard to keep down to only twice a week, were then looked on with suspicion, and investigated.

Naturally, the shit hit the fan, and I was grounded for months, and in big trouble. I pleaded with and begged my parents to keep their hard earned money, and let me out of that school which I hated anyway. The girls were mostly from the very rich and well-to-do families, and the amount of snobbiness and bitchiness was catastrophic. My early hopes of fitting in somewhere were stifled pretty much in my first year at the school. The fact that I lived so far away from nearly 90% of the school's population, didn't help at all. Except for the boarders, and I found out early they stuck together. I had no chance to make any real friends, and I learnt absolutely nothing about life skills there. The only life skill learning was what I discovered in my own way. It was such a waste of precious money my parents didn't really have.

Thank God, they finally relented and allowed me to leave half way through Year 11, which appropriately, back then, was called the Leaving Year.

My next dubious stage of education was at the Holmes Business College. This was situated in Russell Street in the city, a place I knew, by then, like the back of my hand. I was to learn typing, shorthand and bookkeeping. Typing was a cinch, but shorthand and bookkeeping was a real struggle.

It only became apparent to me years later that unfortunately I have a diagnosed condition called "mirror vision". This is simply explained best by imagining looking in a mirror and what you see in the mirror is what I see. That is left is right, and right is left. This rather peculiar and bizarre condition has given me buggery for most of my life in terms of direction, and in other areas where you need to know your left from your right, but particularly hampers my sense of direction.

Needless to say, when someone mentioned to me before a bookkeeping exam at the College, that the debit side of the ledger book was closest to the window in the room, and therefore on the left, it should be a piece of cake to enter the correct figures and total. I attained 15% for my bookkeeping exam and never went back to that class again. I think the 15% was for neatness, (I'm a really neat writer), and quite possibly a bit of sympathy thrown in. I found I also struggled big time with shorthand. All those dashes and squiggles did my head in and I truly hated it.

So off I would go again, wandering the city streets aimlessly, to kill time before I had to catch the tram, train and bus home again in the afternoon, always being careful to avoid the Stock Exchange in Collins Street where Dad worked. I sat in many cafes chatting to all sorts of people, young, old, black, yellow or white, it didn't matter. I used to chat to the homeless too, but in that smart arse attitude way teenagers can have, I didn't really like them much. They scared the shit out of me then. Not sure why, but I couldn't get away fast enough.

Trans Australian Airways was recruiting hostesses back then, and I had a dream of being an air hostess for years. TAA stewardesses always looked so glamorous in their navy blue and hot pink suits, with those long dark gloves, cute hats, perfect skin colour panty hose and navy blue court shoes. It was definitely for me. My Mum and Dad, who I'm sure at this stage, had simply had enough of me and my mucking around, acceded to my wish to train as an air hostess. This involved about twelve months training on flight catering, safety and evacuation, deportment, hair, make-up and grooming, which I actually loved. Finally, I had found something I was pretty good at. I loved talking to people, and was rarely shy.

Nor was I nervous about flying. I could dress up every day, look pretty and travel around Australia for nothing. Seemed like the ideal position for me.

Of course, it became apparent very soon, that I was nothing more than the "glorified waitress," that throw-away line we all have heard, and I suffered the indignity of having my arse pinched many times from drunken footballers on their way home from a match, or worse, old guys who couldn't keep their hands to themselves. The general public were just basically pretty rude. On my feet all day, and tired of incessantly smiling, I gave it away.

I was married within a year.

Chapter 3

At 19 years of age on an exceedingly hot and sultry day in early March, I vowed I would love and honour my husband David till death do us part. The vows taken that day were for me very serious, and deep down in my 19 year old soul, I was determined to stay married till death did in fact part David and I.

My future husband and I had met on a blind date. His Uncle, Aunty and my Mum and Dad were life time friends, and thought David and I could quite possibly be a great match. I was invited to meet David at his parent's home for a meal. I remember at the time, I was a little hesitant, as David's father, Henry was someone whom I had heard quite a bit about, and was a controversial man to say the least. He'd been in the papers for some time, and appeared to be a very large and scary looking man, with an attitude to match. My social life, as it was then, had been pretty quiet, so I thought I might give this "blind date" scenario a try. My Uncle gently pushed me through the front door declaring that he couldn't get a blonde, but I would have to do. I was around 17 at the time, a brunette, thin, and with a flat chest. Although I always put on a show of being confident and pretty sassy at the time, deep down I was dead shy and full of self-esteem issues like any teenager.

David had recently returned from almost 3 years overseas and had only been home for a few short days. It turned out it was his 23rd birthday I was attending. I was his Uncle's birthday gift. He looked really cute but was also very nervous. We did a lot of shy smiling, exchanged many sweet muffled comments, and decided we liked each other enough to continue our relationship.

Sex was something I decided at 15 was a damn fine thing. It also became apparent, that it was something I needed to make the most of, as I had very little freedom at home to explore this glorious adventure. My Dad made sure that I was in my bedroom and well asleep by 8.30 every evening, and even long after I had left school. I was allowed out on weekends but there was a curfew of 11pm, and my life was not worth living if I arrived home one second later.

David and I were like the proverbial rabbits. We just couldn't get enough of each other. We became Mr and Mrs Morris, as David nervously signed the reception papers at pretty much every motel we could find in Melbourne. I would sit and wait in his car scared shitless that they could see inside me, and that we were both lying our horny little heads off. I don't really remember how we afforded the luxury of motel rooms, but we did, and we did it a lot. I even remember a few nights with my legs pressed up against David's Datsun 240Z boot, enjoying the sex that I had become so familiar with. If anyone can remember the old Datsun 240Z's, there wasn't a hell of a lot of room in the back, only boot space! However, at the time these cars were considered very hot cars to own.

David made me feel beautiful and needed. Most importantly, he made me feel safe. He clearly loved me, and I felt I loved him right back, so we thought it was appropriate that we marry. Besides, everybody else was getting hitched, and so why the hell not?

Our parents seemed delighted at the time. On reflection, I think that Mum and Dad, (who by then were living happily in Northern NSW), were just happy I was no longer mucking around with my life, and marriage might just be the ticket to bring me some stability and responsibility. Personally, I think I was simply hand balled.

As David had attended the private school Wesley Baptist Grammar School as a kid, we chose to be married there, and afterwards had our reception at a VFL Social Club. Incidentally, we were wed that day by a Roman Catholic Priest. I wore a gorgeous but simple white bridal gown, and wore flowers in my hair. I carried a sweetly scented bouquet of gardenias. My bridesmaids were in soft blue dresses. The groom and groom's party were in 3 piece blue velvet suits. It was 43 degrees. A great choice.

Our wedding photos were hysterical. The photographer we had chosen never turned up, so my Dad took most of the photographs, and David's cousin also took some. Between the two of them, we had a motley collection of pretty ordinary pictures of our big day. The weather that day stayed as hot and sticky as ever, and although our faces were shiny and sweaty, we looked so damn happy. Which of course we were.

I had spent many years previously learning guitar. My eldest brother Greg, who magically played by ear, had spent a fair amount of time with me teaching me a few basic chords, and he and Angus bought me a guitar for my 13th birthday. I simply loved it. I would play every second I had, with heaps of seconds, minutes and hours spent inside my room practicing and perfecting chords, and picking at the strings to make some semblance of appreciable sound.

On an occasional night, if Greg and I felt it timely, we would go downstairs and put on a little sing-a-long for Mum and Dad. Mum would sit there smiling and full of pride, while dear old Dad would listen very intensely with grimaces and much sucking in of his breath at each note or chord that we may have missed.

I'm not sure if I ever become really proficient at guitar playing, but I did so love sitting quietly in my room strumming away. I wrote lyrics then put music to the words, and found somewhere I could go in my head where nothing and no one could bother me. Greg was good, really good, and we would sit together for hours and play. I got better. We would sing together too, and it just felt right. It was also an opportunity for me to get away from the ever present feeling of being trapped, because when I played and sang to myself, I was as free as a bird.

Although David enjoyed music, he never really listened to me play. He simply didn't enjoy it, and although he certainly was never rude about it, there was a very real feeling that perhaps I should go somewhere else in the house and play, so he didn't have to hear me. I figured at the time that was fair enough. That maybe one day when I got really good, he would love it and want to join in with me. Unfortunately, he believed he couldn't really sing, so was too embarrassed to join in, and on the occasions my brothers or girlfriends would be there, David would find an excuse to leave, or would sit there uncomfortably and fidget. After some years of this I stopped playing. It wasn't something I felt was anyone's fault, it was what it was. My guitar collected dust in the corner of the bedroom for a long time, then was finally relegated back to its grubby old bag and slipped under the bed for years. I grew my nails again, my callouses softened, and I didn't play again for years and years.

Incidentally, before I go on any further with this little book, it is very important that I convey that I was not miserable, nor feeling a deprivation of any sort. It seemed the right thing to do at the time, and I respected David's' feelings. Besides I had 2 beautiful daughters to raise and care for, and there were lots of other things I could be doing.

Many years later I enrolled in watercolour classes. I loved messing around with the water and paint, and watching the colours merge into the water and become something wonderful. I painted and painted. I discovered that I had an affinity with boats. I loved looking at them, sitting in them, sailing in them, but most of all painting them. Seascapes and anything to do with water was studied and put into watercolour. I didn't like painting flowers or landscapes as much as the ocean, a river or a lake.

David and I had a beach house on the Peninsula, and many weekends I would drive down with our Labrador for company, and simply paint. It just made me feel good. I remember one week-end; I had spent a long time painting a scene for David in watercolour. It was a scene reflecting a couple sitting on a jetty, fishing with a boat in the foreground. I thought it was awesome, so I gave it to him as a gift. He said he liked it and he would hang it in his toilet. At the time, I remember I was quite upset. The toilet? Jesus thanks! It was much later I realised that a bloke stands at the toilet 3 to 4 times a day, so he would be looking straight at my painting. That sort of made sense.

David and I were married just shy of 34 years. We had separated twice previously, but reunited with a determination and hope that we could try harder and make it work. After much delaying and postponing, I walked out nearly 4 years ago. He is still a friend of mine, and I would be lying if I said I didn't miss him. How can you not miss someone who has been with you for more than half your life?

We never fought. I can't remember one solitary fight. Maybe we simply didn't care enough anymore to fight for, or about, anything.

We had stopped making love many years before. There was a period in our marriage, that we actually hadn't had any form of intimacy for eight years. What happened? Was there a particular time in our lives when we both just got very sick of each other? Eight years of no intimacy can do your head in. It hurts like hell for months, and then strangely you can just forget about it, and keep going through the paces. Then it comes back again with all the previous hurt and bewilderment.

How we managed to keep going for so long, and stay married is a conundrum. There was never any indication that a third party was involved, and it was only towards the end of our marriage, that I sought solace elsewhere. I'm not proud of this, but it happened. I guess I justified the whole thing as I simply deserved it. I used to equate this justification with food. Simply put, I had been starved and I was damn hungry.

There's nothing new about all this. Marriages end all the time. They end for all sorts of reasons. Some last for years unhappily and die a sorry death. Some of course, last for years and flourish till death. Ours lasted a very long time. We had 2 extraordinarily beautiful daughters of whom we are very proud and they are both fine human beings. We have some wonderful memories and time is a healer.

Chapter 4

After the final separation there comes a time, and in my case, it came very quickly, when that freedom of being single or alone, hits you like a sledge hammer. My first few months of being separated, were surreal.

One might understandably surmise that after being married at 19 for nearly 34 years, I would be relishing a reprieve. A time for solitude and much needed reflection. Maybe even a time to take up a new hobby or a part time job, or maybe a new interest. Nope, not for me. I just couldn't wait to get straight back into the saddle! Reckoned I needed a man and I needed him fast.

Also, the old clock was ticking away sneakily, but very loudly in my head. I was 53 and time was running out.

Jesus, I thought, I don't want to be still doing this shit, and all alone when I'm 60!! I'll be an old woman and no-one will want me then for sure. I'll die alone and loveless. The thought was depressing to say the least.

I was lonely and scared shitless. There was a massive crater in my once safe and secure life which although it had been loveless, was comfortable and very bearable at the time. I was living in a beautiful home, with a garden which David and I had spent many months making superb.

I still remember how I lovingly polished the timber furniture and pieces in that home, and kept it immaculate at all times. It was one of those period homes, with so much charm and character, and was a true delight to live there. I used to watch the light shift throughout the day through the leadlight windows and doors, and marvel at how pretty it all was. I was also lucky enough to be living in an enviable suburb in Melbourne. Life should have been sweet.

I guess I lingered too long. The ostrich with her head in the sand. It's not anything new.

I moved in with a girlfriend, when David and I separated, but only temporarily, while I found myself somewhere to live. She has been my mate for years and she took me in. We had many boozy nights together sorting out the world and me. God bless this woman. She means the world to me.

When I found myself a place to live, I found online dating, and within a few short weeks, I was putting myself out there baring my soul and searching for a man.

Online Dating

The very words themselves are incongruous. Clearly how can one actually meet and date someone by looking at a photo, and reading a profile (which is the carefully or carelessly put together words by the member), and decide if they are worth a looksee? Or an actual first time date?

To really put yourself out there on one of these sites, although anonymously, I believe takes an enormous amount of courage and trepidation. You will have an audience of some 50,000 people or more looking at you, and deciding if you are the chosen one. Your carefully selected photos will be scrutinised, one by one, and the words you took ages to write will be read many times by many, many different people.

I've even noticed that a few women have checked me out? Really!? I know this because on one or two of these sites, they actually let you see who is online at the same time you are, and they also tell you who has been checking you out. Nothing is really private unless you care to spend a heap more money, and become an elite member. This membership will allow you to roam around on the site, and no-one knows you're there. No one will know you've been looking at them. Extraordinary! It does come with a price tag that I personally can't be bothered with, anymore.

Let me tell you a little about these dating sites. I've tried six, yep six of them. They are each of course much the same as the other, although membership fees vary and the method of picking someone, then subsequently chatting to them online can also vary. But they are all basically the same. There are of course others, which seem to be aimed at the sexually frustrated or brain dead and they are possibly perfect for many people.

One has to be pretty astute at picking through the bullshit and the genuine. There are also the sad, bored and frustrated married people, who clearly shouldn't be on there in the first place, cluttering up the works and stuffing things up for many.

I have, over time, become pretty adept at spotting them. They usually like to use words such as "casual dating" as their preference, rather than a relationship, long term or marriage, and call their profile names things like "Only Busty Need Apply", "Lusty Gus" or "Shagging' Time". You probably get the picture.

I had to laugh one day, whilst doing a bit of a search, up popped "Aries the Ram". He actually had an animated picture of a horny ram astride a sheep. How this managed to get through the security gates of the dating sites, I'll never know. They claim to have very stringent rules and regulations about this sort of thing, but thousands of new profiles clearly get passed through daily and quickly. I guess, with over 50,000 single, separated, divorced or widowed people, all signing up and paying the bucks, they just can't keep up with every one of them. I've often quietly thought to myself that there truly are a lot of bloody funny people out there in cyber space who should be on a stage somewhere. They're wasted just being on an online dating site.

My first few dates were horrendous. But being the eternal optimist, I soldiered on with a determination that was enviable. At one stage, I had six lined up in one week. It was inevitable, I would have to forget or mix up their names on the first handshake or kiss, which was never a great start to a date. I became very adept at slipping out of my comfort zone, and actually started to enjoy myself. No longer nervous or shy, I became incredibly confident within myself and perhaps scared most of them away. Overconfidence can be a turn off, I know, but at the time, I couldn't have cared one iota. It was kind of nice to be sought after and admired. Dressing up and going out was a hell of a lot better than the alternative.

My safety was always important to me so I always made sure I had parked my car in a well-lit car-park, or street, ensured I was never followed to the best of my ability, and kept my keys in my hand ready to drive away fast or use as a weapon if necessary. I also made a point of letting someone know where I was going and who I was seeing.

My first "successful" date was with an older man. His name was George and he lived down in one of my favourite places within the Mornington Peninsula. He was as keen as all hell to meet me, as I was to meet him, and we arranged to meet at a lovely restaurant on the beach road.

Fortunately, at the time, David and I still owned the beach house not far away from where George lived, so I spent the weekend down at our beach house. George actually looked like his profile, and he had a way with the words. He turned out to be a very wealthy man, having spent his years as an architect and also a real estate agent, but had clearly made most of his money from designing and building stunning contemporary homes in and around the Peninsula area. He showed me them all proudly, and I was in awe.

He also had a way of kissing that was electric. On reflection, as I had not really done a lot of kissing in my marriage, and the years before then, he could quite possibly have been pretty ordinary. There wasn't much to compare with. However, to me, at the time, it was electric. I decided that I should make him my man. So we had another date, and then another.

The next few months' we spent our weekends together down at his exquisite home complete with an elevator, and 3 levels of spacious living, and me playing wifey. I guess, at the time, it was what I was most comfortable with, so as he strolled out the door at 12.30 to play golf on a sunny Saturday at his prestigious Golf Club, I would spend my afternoon concocting something divine for dinner.

A trip to the overpriced little supermarket nearby for ingredients in the afternoon, followed by much deliberation over how best to cook something simply wonderful for our dinner that evening.

This fella must have thought all his Christmases had come at once!! He had hit the jackpot! Fresh out of a sex drought of many years, I was the veritable whore in bed, looked immaculate and was also a damn fine cook. I never complained, did my nails, sitting in the sun by his perfectly designed swimming pool, keeping my recently powdered nose attuned to the cooking aroma inside, changed my clothes some second or third time to be sure I looked just right as he walked through the door. George would come home, smelling like a distillery, and as happy, hungry and horny as ten men.

I figured what was wrong with that? He told me I was beautiful, he told me he wanted and needed me. That was enough surely? Furthermore, I was still bloody hungry myself.

George had a golf handicap of 2, at the time. A very fine handicap. He and a mate of his flew to Kuala Lumpur to compete in a tournament, for four to five days. We said our sweet goodbyes, with much anticipation of catching up when he returned. He had called me from KL, and everything seemed honky dory.

When George arrived home he simply stopped calling, and to this day, I'm not sure what the hell happened. It was all on, and then it was clearly off. At the time, I was bewildered, as I had thought we had it made. What an empty little shell I was, but it wasn't long before I shook myself off, and was back into the online dating scene.

Chapter 5

One thing with a dating site is that every day, they put up these profiles of people, who some relationship experts have decided are "perfect" for you. It is then up to you to pick one you might like the look of, and send them a "kiss" if you wish. This is the sites' word for sending an email message. Some sites call them "winks".

This is really quite amazing. Particularly as you scroll through the daily update of pictures and profiles.

One day, just for a bit of fun, I pretended I was a bloke, and I did a search of women in the forty eight to fifty five year old category, and was amazed at the amount of work most women had put into their profiles. Generally they would have three or more photos of themselves, pretty as they can be, faces clearly visible, and their figures openly shown and dressed nicely. Most are smiling directly at the camera, and the lighting is good and the picture is easy to see.

I noticed, as I was scrolling down the hundreds of pictures, these same ladies (well the majority of them), had gone to a lot of trouble with their profiles. They write as intelligently as they can, describing what they would like to find in a man, what their interests are, their occupations, and how they spend their spare time, whether they have children or not, and if the children still live at home, and so on.

I too have gone to a lot of trouble to put in relatively recent photos of myself. There are seven photos of me, in all my glory! My profile's words and thoughts are as accurate and as real as I can be, with a decent attempt to reflect as much as I can about myself in a short space. My profile name is probably not that catchy, but I struggled with it for days and finally settled happily with the attempt I'd made.

Allow me to now relate what a woman can find when she decides to go for a little frolic through the thousands of potential males out there in dating land, or as one date I met called it "The Lolly Shop". A funny, but spookily accurate title, I think.

Please understand, the following is not meant as derogatory in any way. Nor does it depict all of the male fraternity on these sites. Some men, I've noticed, put in the exact same effort as it appears most women do, and it's always refreshing to read. It is simply an observation on my part, and very pertinent to the ongoing difficulties with online dating that one can endure.

In addition, I should also mention here, that normally at some point in the early stages of setting up your account and profile, you are asked to fill in what is called your own personal search criteria. This will be reflected on the site, as your own personal prerequisites for age, height, religion (if necessary), approximate locale, and so on, and so on. A bloody good idea too.

I spent quite a bit of time on these particular criteria, as I did have a potential man in mind, and was keen not to get every Tom, Dick Harry, or Larry out there sending me kisses, or winking at me. Some would say she's lucky to get any kisses or winks at all, and they would be right. However, the whole process of the online dating set up takes time, with each and every potential suitor, and nobody has that much spare time to decline the many men or women that you know will simply not work. Hence the ever important deal breakers are set.

In my case, I clearly set down that I did not wish to meet any man under 5'10". Nor did I wish to meet someone who was clearly overweight. Sorry, just don't. However, clearly this had been ignored later when I met the very affable Jerry. The other particular request I put into my deal breaker was that the man I would like to meet, would need to be between 48 and 62. Finally, and I thought it was fair enough, a photo was also a deal breaker. After all I've got 7 of the buggers up there, it's only fair.

By the way I'm not going to go into a great deal of detail as to why I have an aversion to shorter men, (because I guess you might be wondering why). In my experience, (and this is my book, so I get to say this), I have never met a man under 5'10" who hasn't some pretty ordinary issue he's carting around. Usually, a chip on the shoulder about something or other, and generally you as his partner will get to wear and carry around that same chip, at some point or another. This has been my experience, so I figured it's my profile, I might as well make that plain as day from the beginning. This is certainly not to say, that every man under 5'10 has a chip on his shoulder. It has simply been my experience.

So there you have it. A catchy profile name, a neat profile, some relatively attractive and recent photos, and your search criteria and deal breakers clearly stated. Then, if you are not in a particular hurry, you wait and see who might have a bite at your bait. Or if you want to get things moving along a little, in the meantime, you can go on a little search yourself to test the water.

Also, you're single now. You don't have to answer to anyone anymore. You don't have anyone to go out with. Your friends are busy doing other stuff for the moment. You are ripe for the picking and this is precisely what online dating is for.... Yes?

This pastime is sometimes better than telly, I reckon. Let's face it. There's nothing much on the idiot box these days, unless you are into watching another house being renovated, another exotic meal being prepared under scrutiny, another American situation comedy on its sixteenth re-run, or worse another outdated cop show, you just know you've seen before, or even worse again, an unsettling and violent movie, that although you may not have seen before, you sure as hell don't want to look at now.

Yep, and I know we could all be out there doing something else more worthwhile such as regularly pounding the pavement, or volunteering (which I have occasionally done), reading something educational, learning how to play piano (done that to), creating something exquisite in the kitchen (I try). The list goes on and on, but this is sometimes more fun. Not always, and that's for sure, but most of the time it is.

Chapter 6

So there you are. Finally finished work for the day, had your dinner, dishes are dried and put away, a nice chilled glass of wine in your hand, so you sit down at your pc, laptop or tablet and with a few little taps you're "IN". Into the magical, clever, daunting, insensitive, soul-less, amusing, scary, and entertaining world of online dating.

Ah-ha you think, you've had a couple of bites. This is good. Very excited you click on the message which usually says something like, "I like your profile, and would be keen to hear more?" Care to chat?" Innocent enough, and loaded with delightful potential. Told ya it was fun!

You then click on this person's picture and read through his profile. Your initial excitement starts to evaporate very quickly. There in front of you is one, yep just one picture of (well, I'll use one of my many experiences), a man's face generally half covered by sunglasses, a cap to cover his hair or bald head, a distant sunset (pretty), but the light is so dark you can't depict any facial features at all, with a profile that starts with "winning and dinning". This, you get to learn, is a liking for wining and dining. And that is the profile's main gist. There are generally a few words how he loves his Harley or Thumper (I learned that's a Triumph Motor Bike), is into BBQ's and has no baggage.

Baggage is the stuff we have all accrued over our lives which no one really wishes to hear about.

There is generally an undertone, that unless you like to camp out most weekends, lose your kids permanently (if you have them), bonk yourself silly, and of course love winning and dinning .... You might as well take a hike. Oh, and I forgot to mention, that sometimes there is a big spunky photo of said motor bike, in case you hadn't caught on with the blurb.

Oh and by the way, I like bald men. Just would like the opportunity to see exactly if there's hair or no hair. You move quickly on to look at the next kiss or wink you've received.

This is better. There are two photos to look at, so you quickly click on these only to find they're actually one photo put in twice. If you are lucky one of them has been zoomed, so it's bigger than the first one. There is a very sad, clearly troubled man's face with a really catchy profile name like "Happy Harry". I'm not joking. This has happened to me often. His profile blurb will read like the proverbial Peter Pan with an interest in everything including skydiving, all motor sports, night clubs, footy, BBQ's, surfing, and of course winning and dinning.

It clearly becomes apparent that Harry really doesn't do a hell of a lot of that stuff. Crikey, you just know! He's telling porky pies and it's all so very, very sad.

Harry would've done a lot better by putting up a photo of himself smiling, and maybe a couple more of himself and his pet (he said he had a dog), and one maybe of himself doing something he really likes. Harry might be a sad or lonely man, but he would have more chance surely, if he simply told it like it really is.

There are a heap of Harrys out there. Young and old. Women Harrys too.

I believe there is someone out there for everyone.

You have one chance to get it right on this online dating thing, so you surely have to give it your best shot right from the start. By that, I mean a sincere and decent effort to put your best foot forward, be clear, honest and concise in what you are looking for, who you are, and put clear and recent pictures of yourself up there for a potential mate to see.

Now, I need to mention the previously noted "deal breakers". You've already spent a fair amount of time entering these in. They are very important and totally necessary so we can all get what we want out of these sites. There is definitely a time when you will need a break from this exhaustive business, so you want to be able to get what you paid for as quickly as possible, if you get my drift.

Hoping like mad that I don't sound too hard or cynical here. It's not my intention and I'm not actually hard or cynical. I just hate wasting my own time, and other's time.

In my case, the deal breakers I had set were broken every day. I had men under 48 wishing to meet me (yep really), and men over 62 wishing to meet me. I had one little fella who was 5'2" who wanted to know more, and a man who was clearly obese, who thought we were the perfect match

Ok, the men under 48? Hmm, I'd be lying if I said I never looked into this age group. I still believe for me, that is way too young. But I did go on a date with a 42 year old man who had children the same age as my grandchildren. He thought I was Christmas, and I was of course, flattered. Who wouldn't be? He was good looking, fit as a Mallee bull, attentive and wanted a long term relationship, with little old me. So we dated a couple of times.

So there was a problem?

Yes, definitely a problem. I knew, even though he was lovely and all that stuff, I would always see myself as the much older woman, and consequently would never really like myself that much. I'd always be conscious of my impending lack of energy (that he had in spades), and I guess the constant and nagging thought that I would probably end up looking like his Mum one day. So I called it quits. It felt quite sad at the time, because he was a genuine man, and if I'd been 15 years younger, it may have had a chance, but sadly reality was simply staring me in the face. And NO I didn't sleep with him.

If you have the online dating site app set up on your mobile phone, it will emit a lot of beeps and noises from the site or sites you've subscribed. This can be a bit of fun when your phone sounds like you're heating popcorn some days. It sounds like you're really popular, which of course you now are. You are a fresh piece of meat, ready to be picked over, prodded and consumed by every Tom, Dick Harry and Larry.

One of the more popular sites has a top 100 setting. This is simply any member, male or female, who replies to all kisses/emails/winks regularly, whether it be yes or no, has a photo up on their profile, gets a heap of interest from other members, and has their top 100 setting switched on.

I remember how chuffed I was when I actually appeared in the top 100. It is sectioned into age categories and in my case it was the 48 – 55 year olds. I thought I was the Queen of Sheba there for a while, until it became obvious that it is more to do with the amount of responding to interested members that you do. That is, the ones who have sent you messages or a kiss. Even if you don't like the look or sound of any of them, if you have taken the time to respond to each and every one of them, your chances of getting into the top 100 are increased. Damn clever and lucrative for the site itself, but it truly means zilch, as far as you are concerned.

Chapter 7

I was brought up to be polite and mindful of my manners. If someone has sent me a kiss or a message with the words "I like your profile would you care to chat?" I will personally endeavour to respond to each and every one of them. It's simply the right thing to do, I reckon and only takes about sixty seconds or so.

I remember, not so long ago, doing this same thing with a chap who said he'd liked my profile, and would really like to meet me. I sent him some kind words but declined his offer. Before I had had a chance to close down the site for that moment, he responded with the words "So what makes you so fucking special?" Not very pleasant, and also very rude.

Really I should've just moved on and deleted him. You can delete people at any time, or even block them, if they are becoming annoying, or intrusive. However, there was just something about his response that tickled my buttons. Or maybe I had had a crap day. I don't really remember, but I responded with a pleasant enough comment along the lines of "I'm not so special, just doing the right thing here". He then hit me with a barrage of nasties using lines such as "Why don't you just show us your tits, and be done with it?", "You are nothing but a slack arse mole", "You think you're so fucking special don't ya?", and more stuff that I won't bother you with.

It was pretty confronting, and I was quite shocked. This had never happened before.

In fact most of the men I had declined had commented back that they appreciated someone had taken the time to actually let them know and thanked me. So I was quite cheesed off. But this twerp blocked me before I had a chance to dob him in. At one stage he was getting quite nasty and aggressive, so I was thinking I should report him to the site's authorities. But as he had blocked me, I had no proof left to show them, so decided just to move on.

Some days later, I updated my photos on this site, (something I suggest is a great idea from time to time, as it keeps the bait fresh), and clearly he had forgotten who he had abused so badly only days before. He sent me another sweet message asking if I would like to chat with him.

I then had an enormous amount of pleasure letting him know what a pathetic piece of manure I thought he was, and afterwards blocked him. It felt great, although perhaps was childish and immature. But it still felt fantastic!

Online dating can be very successful.

You definitely meet a lot more men or women than you would normally, if you were just going about your business day to day. In an ideal world, we would all like to meet someone at a party, or a social gathering, supermarket, library, pub, art gallery, walking the dog, or just going about our daily lives.

In the cold light of day, this doesn't really seem to happen very much at all. Particularly as one gets older, as we all do.

My 50th birthday was a turning point for me. Although, still ensconced in my marriage at the time, I was very aware of the tick tock of that flaming clock, and also sadly aware that I wasn't going to remain married for much longer.

Chapter 8

Not long after the fiasco with George, I met Jerry online. Jerry was simply charming. A tall, large and gregarious Sagittarian, with a very upbeat personality and an enormous deal of confidence. He had put up his best four photos, and had a profile I could relate to.

Before long, we were chatting on the phone. He had a deep, well-modulated voice which spoke words that literally charmed me to death. Jerry told me that he had some medical concerns, and I was very sympathetic as they sounded pretty ordinary. He hadn't elaborated, at that stage, but I could hear the worry in his voice, and I felt a fair bit of empathy for his troubles.

He had also attended the same school my brothers had, (why that mattered, I'm stuffed if I know, now), and we seemed to have a fair bit in common. I could see from the photos he was very overweight, but he had something indefinable I needed or was very attracted to, so we organised our first date. On reflection, and it's always so much easier to say, "on reflection", but he made me feel safe and very much wanted and needed.

It became apparent that Jerry was not a well man at all. He told me sadly, (on our very first dinner date) that he had a tumour in his stomach, (hence the big gut), and even showed me a small x-ray of it later, after dinner when we returned to his car. Yes it was in his car in the glove box.

The "tumour" was a creamy white colour, rounded and quite large. Having absolutely no experience with what a cancer should look like, I was saddened so much by what I saw. It was a shocker, and he was going to have many overnight stays and trips to the hospital in the near future, to fight the bastard. My first instinct was to give him a big hug (which I'm pretty sure I did), and I further told him that I would be there for him, for support through whatever lay ahead. He told me I was the most beautiful woman he'd ever seen, and had fallen in love with me the first night he set his eyes on me. He continued to use these very same words, throughout our crazy relationship.

I fell for Jerry very hard. To this day, I cannot understand why this occurred. On reflection, I have surmised it could have been simply that I needed someone to take care of. It was a role I was comfortable with, and maybe it just felt right for me at the time. Jerry was in a very bad way, and quite possibly wasn't going to make it, so I stopped seeing anyone else, and concentrated on him and his cancer.

It had also become apparent that Jerry had no immediate family to help. He had a very strange, and estranged relationship with his three sons, and his beloved mother had died some years earlier. His father, although elderly and a pleasant enough man, was not close to him. Jerry had few close friends, and he seemed pretty much on his own.

Jerry lived, at the time, in the city in one of those amazing condominiums up high looking over Melbourne's famous Jeff's Shed. It was quite a large apartment, with a spectacular view over Melbourne and the Dandenong Ranges. I used to love sitting out on the little balcony at night, with a drink and a smoke, looking out at all the pretty lights and colours.

Within a few short months, I had moved in with Jerry. We spent many nights out on the town, dining at all the fabulous restaurants and cafes that our beautiful Melbourne has to offer. From memory, I only cooked a handful of meals, as Jerry was very keen on fine dining, and that's something we did in spades.

After my marriage breakdown, and the few months following, I had lost some weight. Not that I was ever a large woman, as I was always around a size ten to twelve. But clearly as it was a stressful time, I'd managed to lose some weight, and I was comfortably fitting into a size eight dress, jeans or top. I thought I was looking pretty fine.

Within the next four to five months of pretty much eating nearly all of our breakfasts, lunches and dinners out, I was steadily whacking it back on with a vengeance. Jerry had an enormous appetite, and I pretty much kept up with him at the trough. We spent a heck of a lot of time at the South Melbourne Market, and all the surrounding cafes and pubs. We particularly enjoyed the atmosphere, and the cafe life was fun. There would always be musicians playing, and Jerry loved music as much as I did. We also enjoyed heading over to The Crown to listen to the two regular pianists that would play there regularly, and dine at the expensive but very yummy restaurants within that massive complex.

Jerry was too crook to exercise in any shape or form, and apart from slowly making our way from one restaurant, cafe or pub to the next, our exercise was non-existent. He could hardly walk some days as it was so painful for him. However we travelled a hell of a lot, and literally ate our way around Hong Kong, Singapore and parts of the United States of America.

When we were alone together in the apartment, Jerry would sit for hours enjoying the American Wrestling on the TV. I was forever amazed at the many recordings he had of this program, and he watched it whenever he could. Personally, it drove me nuts, all those funny looking men with their steroid bodies gyrating around the wrestling ring, grunting and carrying on. But being a great believer in "live and let live", I didn't get involved, and left him to it.

This was a real shame for a man who had actively played football to a high level at his school and then to an elite standard with an Australian Football League team. His knees, hips and ankles were shot as a consequence of playing hard footy, and also as an athlete in his younger years. He had a very good friend in another chap, called Barry, who had also played for the same team. They would talk to each other daily, using their numbers that they had played with on this team, rather than their names. For example, "G'day 26, 42 here"....

Jerry was a liar, but I didn't know it then. In fact it took me way too long to actually see the truth which had been staring at me all the time.

Jerry was too large to make love to me. I figured it wasn't his fault, as he had this enormous thing growing in his tummy. The tummy kind of got in the way. So we improvised. He also had a passion for my feet. At one stage, I counted close to 175 photos of my much admired feet on his mobile phone.

He really got off on them, and as, by that stage, I had lost all semblance of sanity, I waved them around in front of him, so he could take his photos and get turned on. Sick? Yep it sure was, but I had lost my mind. He was more than happy to pay the $100 or so fortnightly, for me to have them pedicured, painted and prettied up at a very exclusive salon nearby.

Sometimes, when you take a step back in life, and reflect on certain times or incidences that have occurred, which were just so bloody awful, it can hit you like a thunderbolt that perhaps you should've got the hell out of that situation, when you had the chance. Because if you don't, you can question forever, why the hell you bloody didn't? The recurring thought can drive you crazy for a long time.

This was one of these situations.

Jerry and I were on our way home from a weekend in the country. We had visited friends and we were having a massive blue in the car. I believed he had acted like a right prick all weekend, and I was letting him know how I felt about his behaviour, and the problems that had resulted. I had also decided that it was time we called it quits. We simply weren't suited. He was driving me nuts, and I was driving him nuts. It had become increasingly apparent that the more time I spent with Jerry, the crazier I would become. It was time we called it a day.

We had been together about five months by this time. When it was good, it was fun, and sincerely it truly was fun, but when it was bad it was horrendous. Sadly, the bad times were outnumbering the good.

Jerry insisted that we could work it out, and declared his amazing love for me, time and time again.

When we were driving home from the country that afternoon, he became very agitated, when I said I wanted to finish our relationship. He damn near killed us both by driving way too fast and screaming at any driver who happened to pass us. By the time we arrived back at his condo, he was in a hell of a state.

On arrival home I went into the bedroom to start packing up my bits and pieces and get out of there. I had simply had enough.

Jerry was normally not much of a drinker. He'd have the occasional beer, but that was about it.

I didn't realize then that he had grabbed a brand new, large bottle of Bombay Gin from the kitchen, and had drunk the lot in about half an hour. The gin was given to us as a gift from a friend, and had sat in the kitchen unopened for three months. Nor did I notice he had also managed to consume two bottles of wine, whilst I was in the bedroom. He had taken himself out to the balcony, and was cursing at the world and to me, what a shit everything in his life was. It was only after listening to him for a while, I realised he was literally off his face.

He came back inside, at one stage, threw one of my cases at me, and screamed at me to get the fuck out of his life. I was packing as fast as I could, and in hindsight, I probably should've just walked out there and then. It would have been easier enough to come back another day and get my stuff. I should have, right there and then. But I didn't.

He stumbled back out to the balcony and then declared to the world and any poor bugger that was in earshot, that his life was over. That if I left him, there was no point in staying alive. He then screamed out very loudly, he was going to jump off the balcony, and end it all. We lived on the seventeenth floor, so Jerry wouldn't have survived if he did in fact jump. By this stage, he was sitting in one of the little deck chairs we had, and was beginning to become delirious.

At one moment, I thought about grabbing him to try and get him back safely inside, but at 6ft 2" and weighing about 140kgs there was just no way I would be able to do that.

I was scared. I'd never seen him like this before. I'd seen him cranky, sure, but this was a whole new ballgame.

So I called the police. I told them that my partner was threatening to jump off the balcony, was deeply intoxicated, and I needed assistance, fast.

By the time the police arrived, which was only about eight minutes; Jerry was frothing at the mouth and had nearly passed out. The danger of him jumping was gone, but I still needed help.

The police were absolutely fantastic. There were five policemen, and three paramedics, who were able to drag and carry Jerry's heavy frame inside, and on to the sofa, where he proceeded to vomit copiously. They attempted to calm him down, gave him a shot of something, and between four of them managed to carry and drag him out the door, down the elevator and out to the ambulance.

They took him to hospital, and I cleaned up the mess. I also phoned his eldest son to let him know his dad was in hospital, as I thought he should know. Looking back, I was probably acting in automatic pilot, and quietly felt I needed to do the right thing. I was still intending to leave that night.

To this day, I'll never understand why I didn't. There was justification and I certainly had the perfect opportunity.

I remember I was very tired, and figured they would keep Jerry in overnight for sure. I figured that his stomach would need to be pumped, and he would need observation for some time. Therefore I could leave in the morning before he arrived back, so I took myself off to bed.

Some hours later, from memory around 2.30am, the buzzer was going off right next to the bed, indicating a visitor downstairs. On answering it, I heard Jerry's voice, still very intoxicated, pleading to let him in, how sorry he was, and full of his usual declarations of love for me.

He had discharged himself from the hospital, and caught a cab home. He needed money for the driver and he wasn't going away. I let him in and gave him the money for the driver. Although he had sobered up a little, there was no point in talking to him that night, and he fell into a deep sleep.

The next morning, Jerry was a different man. He seemed very remorseful, and loving. The words he used to dissuade me from leaving were so poignant that they hit a raw nerve. We talked and talked, and for some extraordinary reason, I chose to stay.

Not too long after, as we both had a love for the Peninsula area, we went halves in the purchase of a stunning home at Mt Eliza. Complete with an impressive view to Arthurs Seat, Port Phillip Bay, and on a clear day you could see Portsea, and some days, even the high rises of Melbourne. It had a magnificent landscaped garden, something I had missed dreadfully since my marriage, and we moved in very quickly and set up home. I loved that home, and still miss it terribly.

There came a time with Jerry, I became a little suspicious about his glorified and overblown comments to all and sundry, regarding his previous football involvement and history. Things just didn't add up.

It also started to piss me off, as Jerry would find any opportunity to tell just about everyone we met, from the milk bar proprietor, to the lady serving us drinks at the local racing club, about his glorious football past and achievements.

You may question here, why it took me so long to catch up? Great question and it's one that I still ask myself many times. It's unbelievable, how I simply shut down, and blindly wore those bloody big blinkers on my head, like those superb Clydesdale horses.

Jerry had a vast collection of sporting history books in our bookcase. One in particular, was a book dedicated to every single football player that had EVER played footy for Jerry's club. I searched through the entire book from front to back. There was absolutely no mention of him.

I then found another bigger book, similar to the previous one, but with more pictures and a vast history again of these elite footballers. Still zip on Jerry.

I knew his very good friend Barry had played in the same team. He was a well-known VFL player at the time. Barry was in those books, with pictures and details of his success and near Brownlow Medal status. He clearly wasn't telling any porkies.

I remember an occasion when I actually asked Barry if Jerry had played with that same VFL footy team, and he would give me a distorted, sort of muffled answer, but it was always in the affirmative. These two guys were as thick as thieves; they called each other every second day, and clearly had been friends for years.

I still wonder today what Jerry had on Barry? I really liked Barry. He was a genuine, sweet guy and he had a lovely partner, in Annabelle. Jerry and I had many BBQ dinners and lunches with this couple, and always had a fabulous time.

When I asked Jerry why he wasn't mentioned in the books, he told me how, at some point in his life, he had a female stalker who had apparently one night, tried to break into his apartment with a pair of scissors to stab him. Although the police had been involved at the time, it was hard to prove, but she had had an intervention order to stay away from Jerry.

He then advised me that that was the reason his name wasn't in the books. He didn't want her to be able to contact him again. At the back of one of these books, there was a long list of former player's names and details, and Jerry had somehow managed to get to the publishers of these books and have all reference to him deleted.

Now any idiot could've seen through this lie pretty damn quickly. My blinkers were still stuck on my head, and I swallowed it up. Another lie.

On another occasion, not long before I had my epiphany, Jerry and I had planned a trip to Perth together. His youngest son was getting married over there. At this stage in our relationship, I was well on my way to leaving him. It seemed a bit ordinary for me at the time to travel to Perth with a man I didn't really care about anymore, so I told him I didn't want to go at the last minute. Sure, it was a bit thoughtless on my part, to leave it so late, but I wasn't too rational at the time.

Jerry ended up going on his own, but not too happily. However, I had four peaceful days and nights on my own in the house. One afternoon, while he was in Perth, I needed my passport number for a form I was filling out, and went to the bedroom to get it. It wasn't there. I turned the bedroom upside down looking for it, then the living room, kitchen and every damn cupboard and drawer in the place. No passport. It was really odd that I couldn't find it. It was in a distinct pink leather wallet, and had been in the same place for months.

When I spoke to Jerry next, I mentioned it. He said he hadn't seen it, and didn't know where it could be. He also became very annoyed that I persisted in questioning him.

There were also, I thought, some discrepancies with my bank account. Nothing too serious, but at one stage, I went looking for my recent bank statements. Funny, the file they were in was missing too. It was just bizarre. They were there only a few short days ago, I knew, because I remembered seeing them. Jerry didn't have a clue where they were either.

A couple of weeks later I was downstairs in the store-room just off the carport, where we kept garden equipment, suitcases, and other bits and pieces. Right up the very top ledge, was a black suitcase of mine, which I thought could come in handy. I climbed a little step ladder and grabbed it, thinking it seemed a bit heavy for an empty suitcase.

I opened it up and there was my pink leather wallet with passport, and a file containing all my bank statements. I was bewildered and very angry, and headed back upstairs to confront Jerry.

He hotly denied any knowledge of how these two items managed to get themselves into my old black suitcase and fly up to the top of the ledge in that store-room.

There was just no way he would tell me the truth. Nobody else would have moved them, it was so obvious, but old Jerry was sticking to his guns.

I'm not sure why he would have done it in the first place. Did he think I was going to leave the country? And as for the bank statements, that still remains a mystery. Everything seemed to be fine with the recent transactions, and nothing seemed out of the ordinary.

Jerry and I didn't last much longer.

I guess, at some point, I had an epiphany and after finding my senses with the much appreciated help of family and friends, I made plans to leave him. I very much wanted and needed my half share back from the house, so proceeded to square that with his father. I had ascertained earlier, at some stage that Jerry had very little money of his own, and it was his father who drip fed him substantial amounts monthly into his bank account. Fortunately, his father, who was a decent bloke, returned my half share in the house, minus the Stamp Duty, and I was free to leave.

I picked an opportunity when Jerry was having his first knee replacement done in a nearby private hospital. He had embarked on a hospital journey to have the other knee replaced, then his ankles, and finally his hips in the next 12 months or so. Jerry seemed to be at his happiest, when he was in a hospital. With nurses and doctors attending to his every need in his own private room, I swear that man was in heaven.

He had spent the previous few months controlling where I was going, and who I was seeing, so I waited patiently till he had to go to hospital, then quickly organised a moving van and got myself out of there.

I remember, many times I had expressed a desire to travel down to Melbourne and see my daughter and my 2 little grandchildren. I was keen to visit them, at the very least, weekly. Jerry was not too comfortable with this, but relented eventually. However would then send me texts and call me constantly when I was with them. I remember, after already giving him a final hug by my car, and finally making my way down the road towards the freeway, my mobile would ring, and there would be Jerry asking if I was OK, and to have a safe drive, and a great time. All that stuff, we had just 3 minutes earlier, said in great detail. It was awful. Sometimes, he would call me another 2 – 3 times, as I was driving the hour long journey to Melbourne.

I have no doubt Jerry loved me, but it was an all-consuming love that can slowly suffocate and kill any semblance of rational thought you might once have had. Jerry probably never really saw it coming, and at the time, I really needed every ounce of energy and courage to get out of that house.

I'm glad I did.

Jerry's cancer was never cancer. He had a large polyp which was removed quickly and cleanly. Jerry also never played football for that elite football club, except for one night game with an under 19 side. Jerry was not a wealthy man; he lived off his father and probably still does. He hadn't worked at any particular paid employment for years and years.

Jerry's kids didn't like him very much, as he was a self-centred man who had had some very ordinary struggles with a nasty addictive drug some years earlier, before I met him. This addiction had caused many years of troubles and dramas for those kids of his that I now totally understand where they were coming from. At the time, I felt so sorry for Jerry. I don't anymore. There was so much of Jerry that was such a lie, that even today I'm still sickened and sad that I was so weak and vulnerable that I had fallen into his web.

Should probably add here, that I really couldn't have cared less if Jerry was once an elite footballer and or athlete, nor did I care particularly if he was wealthy or not, but the fact that he carried these lies constantly, and used them at various social gatherings over and over again, was what made me so very pissed off. As for the blatant lie regarding his life threatening cancer, that was the lowest of low.

Apparently, Jerry has a new lady by his side now, and I believe she has moved into the Mt Eliza home with him. I hope she's ok, whoever she is.

No-one should ever have to go through what I did, as a woman who was wide eyed, trusting, fresh out of a long marriage, vulnerable as all hell, and clearly as dumb as shark shit.

Jerry was a classic sociopath.

I've added some excellent "words of wisdom" regarding sociopaths at the end of this book for anyone who may find themselves in a similar situation that I was with Jerry. The information I have given is a very brief outline of a classic sociopath. A more detailed analysis can be found in the book "The Sociopath Next Door" written by an American psychologist and author Martha Stout. I have extracted some of the personality traits, behaviours and basic signs to be aware of.

It was time for me to toughen up.

Chapter 9

There was an opportunity to rent a townhouse near my daughter and grandchildren, and I grabbed it quickly. It is literally a 3 minute walk from my front door to hers.

Sadly, during my time with Jerry, my relationship with my daughters had weakened badly, and I was very keen to mend the bridges. To be able to live near my family was wonderful, and although I was a pretty sorry mess emotionally back then, having them so close by was truly a godsend.

My time with Jerry had left me in a pretty bad way. I was definitely going through depression. I felt the very best of me had been stolen, and I had lost it forever. I felt my worth was zilch. I had sought professional help and it took some time before I felt well again.

I spent many hours with my beautiful grandchildren in the following months, and with the help of my gentle, and very wise brother Greg, my daughters and friends, I started to slowly come good.

My darling brother Greg actually rode down from Northern NSW on his motor bike, when I first moved back to Melbourne, to help me feel better about myself.

Every girl should have a brother like I have. He's been there for me through it all, and I love him to the moon and back.

There then was finally that long period of quiet reflection and solitude. I lost weight gradually, easy to do, as I had little appetite, walked my little dog a heck of a lot around the gorgeous green reserves nearby, and spent quality time with my grandchildren.

Online dating had been put on the back bench, but not for too long.

At some stage later, I was introduced to a Greek man, through some mutual friends. He was a very tall, fit, and attractive man who was a

Scorpio. He didn't have a hair on his tanned body, with a lovely, shiny scalp, and a great smile. He also lived about a 15 minute drive away. He was roughly my age, we both had a love for similar music, and hallelujah he turned out particularly awesome in bed!

I figured that things maybe, were finally going to get better for me. I played as hard to get as I could in the first few weeks, but he was a persistent and persuasive fella and I just liked the look of him. The fact that he was previously in law enforcement probably was the clincher. I took him on.

Just have to love a man in a uniform huh?

Nicko … or Nick, as he liked to be known, had a dark side, but I didn't know that then.

If I had paid any attention to astrology, which I do, but only for a bit of fun, I may have realised that a Scorpio and a Gemini have actually little chance of connecting at all. Scorpios are particularly known for their incredible depth and passion and can be very intense personalities. They love power and are full of mystery. Very attractive. Whereas, Geminis, are as flighty as all hell, and rarely take things too seriously at all. We like to keep things light and airy, however we can be serious when the time is right.

He took me out for dinner a couple of times, but clearly preferred to cook for me at his home. The food he cooked was always really tasty, and I enjoyed our nights together very much. After dinner, we would go out on his lovely balcony, overlooking a huge sportsground and reserve, and sip a lot of red wine and talk and talk for hours. He was an intelligent, man with a very quiet manner, and a wacky sense of humour. With a smile that could light up a room, it wasn't long before we were in his bed doing what comes naturally.

In the beginning, he was an incredibly attentive lover, and although I never slept the whole night there, I could imagine myself eventually, falling more deeply for Nick, and staying over a little more often.

Nick had a security position at a nearby large hospital, and worked shifts. He worked a hell of a lot of these, which was fair enough. In the beginning of our short relationship, I figured he was a dedicated employee and was on a pretty good income.

One night, after we had been to a rare social gathering, he invited me back to his home for a drink and a little slow dancing. Always so lovely. At some stage in the evening, while we were listening to some gorgeous music, I was sitting next to him on the sofa. He took my hand, and guided it down his jeans. Now, I've never been a big fan of this, as I like to do this sort of thing when I'm good and ready, but I obliged on this occasion.

My first thought, at the time, was his tackle felt particularly smooth. I clearly had been there before, but this time, it felt very different. On further exploration, I discovered a little lace under my fingertips. Particularly sober now, I explored a little further, and had a little look. There in front of me were the prettiest, lacy knickers I've ever seen. Remember the old "Laura Ashley" print?

Well, Nick was wearing panties with a similar print.

A few weeks earlier, Nick had said to me in all seriousness that one should dress from the inside to the out. In other words, one should pay particular attention to your bra and panties, before dressing further. I really wish now, that I had listened to the warning bells sounding in my head, at that time. He had even offered to take me lingerie shopping as soon as we both had the time.

My hand shot out of his fly like it was on fire.

With some dumb comment like "what the hell?" I stared open-mouthed at Nick. He quietly and simply asked me if I liked them. I said something even dumber like, "I think they would probably look better on me". To which he added that we would have to get a larger size. Charming!

I think I was in my car within 60 seconds, and half way home. I didn't speak to Nick again. It bothered the hell out of me, at the time. On further reflection, it was probably a little careless on my part, and perhaps rude. I simply left with no explanation.

It was just such a shock. Here's this tall, very manly ex-copper in lacy panties. Any desire I had for him disappeared in seconds, and I just couldn't get it going again.

Some months later, while I was enjoying a week's holiday up north with my brother Greg and his lovely partner, Caroline, I received a text from Nick asking if we could get together for a drink. He wanted to make amends and have a bit of a chat. Thinking back, I probably should have given it the big A, but I did have a little guilt that I had been quite rude that night, so I accepted. Put it down to my upbringing I guess. Good manners cost nothing.

Nick and I had our drink and chat, at a local pub, and I later told him that provided he wears the right underwear from now on I'd be happy to give it another go. We had a good old laugh about the whole thing, and were back on track.

Not long after, Nick asked me if we could be exclusive. After much thought, I accepted and for about 2 weeks things seemed ok. It was a funny kind of relationship though, as Nick worked more and more shifts, and when he wasn't working he was too tired for much else. We rarely went out anywhere, because he was so tired all the time, and the only time I would really see him was at his home for one of his tasty dinners and of course bed.

Nick amazingly became less tired when it was bedtime. He had the energy and stamina of a man half his age sexually, and he would go from a slow, red-eyed, and tired 50 years plus man to a veritable teenager in the sack. There were a couple of activities he seemed to relish just as he was about to orgasm.

Right at that exquisite moment, he would grab a large handful of my hair and pull it as hard as blazes back from my head, and then literally smack me hard on the arse. Any orgasm I might have enjoyed went straight out the window. It bloody hurt! I kept telling him not to do this, but he kept doing it anyway. Not sure if this is a Greek thing, as I'd never slept with a Greek man before. And it's probably not something you can just ask somebody, anyway.

As he had only recently asked me to be exclusive with him, I always thought that he would at some point make a better effort. I'm still, to this day, bewildered after a phone call I had made to him, where I suggested we should perhaps have a little chat regarding some issues we clearly were having.

I had sat quietly at home, one afternoon, and carefully wrote up a pros and cons list of Nick's traits and mine. There was nothing in that list of mine, which would have been impossible to conquer. We actually seemed to have a very good chance of being a great couple. He had asked me previously to be as honest and upfront with him as I wanted, and if I had any concerns to let him know, and we could simply work things out.

Nick never actually got to hear what those issues were, but simply surmised that I was having a go at him, and later sent me a vitriolic and really nasty text implying I was too controlling and self-centred. Our rather short and tumultuous relationship was well and truly over.

I'm pretty sure it was already over for Nick, long before I knew about it.

To this day, I believe that honesty in a relationship is quite possibly the most important thing.

Without this, you really have no foundation to build on.

If Nick didn't want me, he really should've told me. Perhaps he was simply waiting for the right opportunity, when I phoned that day.

Nick has long gone from my mind, and I haven't seen him since. Surprising, particularly as he lives quite close to me.

However, funnily enough, Nick unwittingly, had done me a massive favour. I realised my sense of humour was well and truly back and intact, when I had a damn good chuckle to myself about what an idiot I had been.

Chapter 10

My confidence was back surprisingly. I felt stronger, and less needy. I had lost weight, I made lists, and I had a sense of worth again.

However, I was still alone. And alone was not what I wanted. Still isn't.

One of the things I've always enjoyed doing is giving someone a massage. I've always been a pretty tactile person I guess, so I enrolled in a college for 6 or so months and did a Massage Therapy course. They even threw in a massage table which saved me about $300. The college was easy to get to, and I started in early March. Anatomy and Physiology, Body Development and Organisation were some of the subjects we needed to learn, and there were many classes necessary, also, to learn the practice of the various massages that people enjoy today.

I had sucked at school, and I had sucked at Business College. There was a very real fear for me, that I would most likely suck at this. We had exams weekly and Physiology and Anatomy were subjects that were very intensive, and hardly a piece of cake. I studied my arse off. When I wasn't at the college, I was home studying hard.

Used to get quietly pissed off too, as I thought there was way too much information to learn simply to massage someone. I was in for a rude shock. Massage therapists obviously need to know a hell of a lot about the different muscles, joints, ligaments, and bone structure of the body. You clearly can't expect someone to pay you good money, if you don't really have a clue what you are doing. So I worked harder than I ever have in my life, to pass each and every exam. There were so many, but I passed them all. Some were just passes sure … but a pass all the same. I was ecstatic! Finally, here's something I can do, and even make a quid.

So, for 6 months or so, I hadn't dated. I didn't miss it at all. Obviously there wasn't a hell of a lot of time anyway for me to date, but I simply didn't think about it.

Now I'm a qualified massage therapist, and even have my graduation ceremony next month. So, I'm not studying anymore, I have time ....

I decided that two dating sites have got to be better than one. So I joined another, and set up my profile and photos again. Although picked photos that were different to the other site I'm on.

Pretty quickly, I had a few bites. One in particular stood out.

Tall, tanned and clearly well spoken, with a smile that spoke volumes. We chatted backwards and forwards for a while, then arranged to meet for dinner. It was a lovely date, and we seemed to hit it off. His name was Roger and he lived in Whoop Whoop, which was a bugger, cos it was miles from me.

Seems to be the way for me, if I finally find someone half way interesting or cute and with some potential, they either live interstate or are a long drive away, where you will need to pack a lunch to eat while you drive.

We arranged to meet about halfway one sunny Sunday afternoon for a late lunch, and I listened to this man chat intently and enthusiastically about his business. He was an Artificial Inseminator for Top Class racehorses. His job was probably pretty mucky, but he was getting paid the big bucks to inseminate horses with the superior stuff to make quality racehorses. He'd obviously had a shit of a marriage, as he told me all about it on our second date, but was keen to get cracking again.

I simply liked him. Nothing more and nothing less. There were no bells clanging away or gushes of euphoria, but he had something I liked and I wanted to see some more. One night, not long after, (I think it was our fourth date), I invited him back to my home for a coffee after a movie we'd seen. We were simply sitting around chatting and we started talking about Chinese Astrology. You know the meaning behind which year you were born such as The Year of the Dragon I think is 1952.

We had both had a couple of good reds by then, and feeling quite relaxed, and Roger asked me what year I was .... Then I asked him what year he was etc. He told me, then excused himself to go to the toilet. I did some calculations .... Not my strongest talent, but added it all up. This very fit and wiry man would have to be about seventy three! When Roger returned I quickly asked him what year he was born and it confirmed my calculation. He was close to eighteen years older than me! I became a little cranky, as that was a big fib, but he remarked that he felt more like a 30 year old.

Roger and I parted that night, not very well. I just couldn't get over the age thing. I know it's wrong, and one shouldn't judge, but he had lied with a biggie there, and then of course you start thinking hm.... what else you might be fibbing about? Perhaps if he had told me earlier it may have made a difference. I'm not sure ...

Chapter 11

I was dead keen to get back on track again, so dated some more men who seemed nice and normal on the site. Nice and normal is often hard to find. But Zip! There simply was nobody out there for me at that time. It is an exhausting process, and you can lose hope daily.

It is often the way that the ones you like, don't want to know you, and the ones you're not too keen on, reckon you're the ant's pants. I'm sure this is the way for many. I wouldn't be alone at all with this reckoning.

However, I have always been a fairly optimistic lady, so I continue on my search.

One day while cruising around on one of my dating sites, I saw a vaguely familiar face. Not that I felt I had known that face personally, it was simply a feeling I'd met him somewhere before. After reading his profile and looking at his face for a little while longer, I realised straight away who he was.

A very well-known AFL player, who was always in the sporting papers back in the 80's. He was considered a bit of an eccentric and a very snappy dresser.

We actually seemed to hit it off on the chat line, and followed up soon after with a few phone calls.

His name was Dennis and we arranged to meet and have a few drinks and a meal in the city.

I really didn't know much about this man, except his past football glories, but figured that it would make for a great evening, just listening to him talk about his past experiences and, also with the press, which he'd clearly had quite a bit to do with at that time.

Dennis arrived at the table in deep green trousers, a bright red long sleeved shirt, red shoes and wearing an orange, yellow and green bandana on his bald head. His fashion sense was truly "out there", but he did seem to carry it with much aplomb and swagger. He was very tall, probably close to 6ft 5", and as physically fit as any man half his age. He truly was in fine shape.

He and I sat there for a while chatting and eating .... And while I was looking at him chatting away, I remembered something a little scary, I had read in the papers some years earlier.

Dennis had been arrested for physically abusing his partner at that time, and although I don't know the sorry details, or the outcome, I then became a little fidgety.

From then on, the night became a distant memory. I was as keen as all hell to get home as fast as I could. Dennis intimated he was dead keen to come back for coffee, and probably more than I had bargained for.

Now, to be fair, Dennis may have paid his dues back then, and of course, I only knew what I'd read in the papers, which aren't exactly gospel, but any semblance of a relationship with this man was evaporating fast.

I actually called on the old "I'm feeling a migraine coming on, must have been something in the food" excuse, and begged off. I must be a great actress, as he did believe me. He walked me to my car, and after I gave him a very quick peck on the cheek, I drove away as quickly as I could.

A couple of days later in the Sunday papers, there was a picture of Dennis and I sitting having dinner that night, and some peculiar comments about his sexuality, and his fashion sense. I have no recollection that anyone had taken our photo that night. Obviously someone from the press was there at some stage.

For the next few weeks, Dennis called my mobile number daily. I didn't answer.

I was sure to block him as quickly as possible from the dating site, so that should have been the end of it.

Dennis was apparently bi-sexual, with which incidentally, I have no problems.

Each to their own, I reckon. It was his violent past that had freaked me out.

Not long after, I answered a sweet message from a man who turned out to live just 10 minutes away. He spoke nicely and was very well presented. We arranged to meet at a well-known cafe nearby for coffee. He told me he would be sitting outside, and I couldn't miss him, as he had a lot of silver hair. I remember doing a drive-by, and seeing a chap with very silver hair, sitting outside the cafe reading a newspaper.

At first, my instinct was to keep driving. Because from a distance, I felt sure that this bloke was also

a lot older than he stated. Sure as hell wasn't going to go through the same disaster I'd just experienced with Roger. I changed my mind. Parked my car and walked towards him. Incidentally, I would probably never actually keep driving. That is just plain bloody rude, and I really have never done it. Ha but I've thought about it. However, I'm sure glad that I didn't.

Jack turned out to be a darling. Although instinctively, I knew straight away, Jack wasn't boyfriend material, he was simply one of the nicest people I've ever met. And to be fair, I don't think I was going to be girlfriend material for him. Jack is still one of my best friends, and he and I have spent many hours chatting and laughing about this dating business.

He's the sort of guy you want on your team. He's confident, affable, funny, but sensitive when the need arises. In fact it's a conundrum that Jack hasn't been snapped up by now. He's a very tall, good looking man with the best attitude of anyone I know.

Chapter 12

Ahhh, Neil. We met on my older dating site, the one that I'd been on for a couple of months. Neil's' photos were attractive, his profile read well and he was also as keen to meet me, as I was to meet him. He was a Leo, and although a little younger than me, I saw some potential. We arranged to meet for lunch and we both arrived at exactly the same time.

Neil had a problem. Neil simply had verbal diarrhoea. It would not be a lie that from the very moment we sat down and ordered a bite to eat, to the finish of my coffee, Neil never drew breath. He literally could talk under water with a mouthful of sand.

I was lucky enough to learn every single thing, in the greatest detail about Neil. I listened to his voice and watched his lips move. Neil didn't leave anything out. I heard about his first marriage, and then his next. How his wives were pure evil and still are. How his kids can't stand their mother and that most of his mates have the same problems as he does with their ex-wives. I heard about the day he bought his first car, the problems he'd suffered at school, his elder daughter's addiction to drugs, and his other daughter's anorexia issues, how his boss is a right bastard, and just doesn't understand him. How he loves to water ski, and should have been in the top 10 skiers in the country if it wasn't for his crook back.

I distinctly remember thinking about what I would get myself for dinner that night from a nearby supermarket, and if I'd have time to walk my dog before dark, as he was rambling on about the bastards he has to work with, and if his superannuation will cover his future hopes. It was just awful.

Neil doesn't know a thing about me. Except for my first name, and what he must have read on my profile. He didn't ask me one solitary question. You may say, perhaps he was nervous? You know, sometimes, when you're nervous or anxious, you can prattle on and on …..! I thought about this while watching Neil's' lips move, and decided Neil wasn't nervous at all. He just liked to talk, and talk he did.

At some point, I interrupted Neil, touched his arm briefly, and said that I'd heard enough, and perhaps at some point, if he was on another date, he might like to ask that person something about that person. I excused myself, paid the bill and kept walking. I looked back for a second, and Neil was still sitting there, with his mouth open.

Was I rude? Yeah probably. But it made me so cranky.

As much as I like to chat away with nearly anyone, surely it's a two way street.

I came home from my date with Neil, and quickly deleted him.

Then there was Colin.

Colin was a smoothie on his profile, and looked pretty good. He had this dark wavy hair, and an impish smile. We both arranged a date in Camberwell. Oh yep, he was a Gemini too. Same as me. This, I figured could work, you just never know.

As soon as I sat down after the initial handshake and kiss on cheek, I knew something was not quite right. Colin unfortunately had a bad stutter. Now I'm never sure the etiquette with a stutterer. Do you put them out of their misery and finish the bloody sentence for them, or do you watch them squirm with embarrassment as they struggle to finish? Not sure, but I did the latter.

It was a long date, and although Colin seemed like a nice enough fella, I just couldn't go back for seconds. I had made an effort, as best as I could to make Colin relax, and I cracked a few jokes, hoping that they might help. They didn't. He just couldn't get his words out and jammed on many. He didn't seem, at any stage, to become more comfortable, and the more he talked to me, the worse he became. It was disappointing, as he clearly couldn't get comfortable with me. I sincerely hope Colin has sought some help to conquer his stuttering …. As he really did seem like a normal, well-adjusted and decent man.

Next? Tony.

Tony somehow managed to check my Facebook page, and business page and he had obtained my mobile number. He'd firstly checked me out on the dating site, and chatted to me there, then proceeded to chat to me via my business email, and then my private mobile number. I had actually asked Tony just to stick to the online chat but he didn't get the message, and continued to infest my personal and private business pages.

He looked very attractive on his profile, and was very insistent that we were most definitely perfect for each other. We just need to meet. He was already making plans for our future before our date. It was crazy. What the hell was I thinking?

I met Tony at a great pub nearby.

Have you ever met someone in your life, male or female that has an attitude, and a face you just want to smack? Probably only 1 or 2 people in your entire life may bring on this inclination. Tony had that face. He had that attitude too. From the very moment, he opened his mouth to speak, I wanted to deck him. Not that I really would, but you know what I mean.

We actually ended up having a fight right there amongst all the families and friends having dinner at their favourite pub on a Friday evening. He had more front than Myer. He believed that it was considered a pretty desperate thing for a woman at my age to be on dating sites, and now I had met him, it was time for me to get off them. After all, he said, he'd be pretty much doing me a favour. Oh yep, he also mentioned that I was lucky I was still pretty, cos otherwise it would all be pretty gloomy for me.

There was just so much stuff that came out of his mouth; it was like the sound of long nails scraping down a chalkboard to me. He had already paid for our dinner, and my good manners were still intact, so I sat there for a little while longer, and listened. I asked him how long he had been on the dating site for and I also asked him how long he had been divorced. Tony was divorced 10 years ago, and he's been on dating sites ever since.

I let him have both barrels. I just couldn't help it. Tony copped a rather nasty barrage of comments from me, that maybe he didn't deserve, but he pushed every single button I had. So I let him cop it!

Quickly downed my coffee, and walked out. By the time I was half way home, I was nearly wetting my pants, I was laughing so hard.

Next day, I had a text from Tony.

He had decided after much deliberation, that even though I was one of the most argumentative, and confrontational women he'd ever met, he would very much like to see me again. No bull shit!!

You've got to have a laugh. A sense of humour is an absolute must.

If you took everything literally that you hear from the mouths of some people on these dates, you would sink into depression for sure, or slash your wrists at the first opportunity.

Chapter 13

I have met some lovely people. I have met some very kind, good wholesome human beings. I have also met some very lonely people, who may have tricked up their pictures and profiles, but they also have a story to tell.

I am lonely. There are nights I can have, where I feel like I'm the only person in the entire country still alone on a Saturday night. There are nights also, I'm glad to be alone. I can do what I like, eat what I like, or not eat, read as late as I like. There are also nights, I'm cranky or sad, and I think it's just as well I'm on my own, as I'd be shit company, anyway.

However, most of the time I'm not so much lonely, as alone.

I have some good friends, (thank God), a lovely family, the sweetest little dog ever to keep me company and I sure as hell, am better off than a lot of people. I know that, and I'm grateful.

I wrote on a pad, about 18 months ago, some words that resonated with me at the time. I stuck them on my fridge and look at them nearly every day. It was around the time, I'd returned to Melbourne after my relationship with Jerry and I have tried to stick to those words as best as I can.

Be Brave. Be Strong. Be Grateful. Be Kind. Be True.

Being brave is exactly what you are doing each time you set out your front door and off to another date. It's very brave, and I was very brave when I met Daniel.

Daniel (a Gemini) actually lived south of Sydney. (Typical). We had connected on the dating site, and hit it off immediately. I liked the way he spoke, who he was, what he was looking for, and he was also damn attractive to me. He had business in Melbourne so we organised a dinner together.

Our first date was wonderful. Daniel ticked every damn box of mine, and, he liked me a lot too. We arranged another date soon after and bingo – we liked each other a lot more. We had another coffee together before he went back to NSW, and I was very attracted to this tall, quietly spoken, fair haired man. He was originally from Melbourne, but had moved to Sydney with his wife and children many years earlier.

Fast forward many months, and Daniel has persisted with his desire for me to travel there and stay with him for a few days, is phoning me regularly, and texting gorgeous words.

I knocked him back a couple of times, because it just seemed way too soon for that, suggesting that perhaps we should meet again, next time he was in Melbourne for business.

Anyhow, I finally agreed to go.

This man had built himself a delightful cabin in the coastal woods, near the Shoalhaven area. It was very high up in the hills, overlooking the bay. Absolutely heaven. It was miles from anywhere really, and I remember the drive up the very windy and later bumpy dirt road to his cabin, took forever. The cabin itself was fabulous, with every mod con imaginable, and he had furnished it beautifully.

Brave.

I went with my gut instinct and we booked my flight to Sydney. Daniel was going to meet me at the airport, and we would drive the 3 hour trip south to his home.

Brave.

I have never done anything like this before in my whole life. Here I am a woman in her mid-50; flying interstate to see and stay with a man I had only met 3 times, and really didn't know that well. It was pointed out to me by some, that he could have been a nutter, or a murderer and I'd be a sitting duck.

Brave.

Because I actually went.

It was the best thing I could have done.

Daniel and I had the most wonderful time together high up in those hills, in that lovely cabin of his. He was the perfect gentleman, and couldn't do enough for me. He cooked me breakfast, and lunch. He took me out for delicious dinners and he also cooked some mouth-watering meals for me at night. We listened to Mozart and the Eagles, and we talked constantly.

We made love, and were deliriously happy for 5 days. He even shampooed my hair, while I was showering on his enormous deck with a big shower rose set up for wonderful, hot outdoor showers.

Now this is a pretty massive thing for a woman in her mid-50. After all gravity is not our friend at all. Hell, I still have issues with donning a bathing suit and sitting on a beach. But right there, with all my bits and pieces clearly out there in the broad, gorgeous sunlight, I allowed and subsequently loved the fact that David washed my long hair beautifully with his herbal shampoo and conditioner.

The very fact that I stood there under that shower spoke volumes to me. I completely trusted this lovely man, and just let it all happen. Even today, I wouldn't have changed a thing.

He set up a massage table in the sunshine, complete with discreetly laid towels to cover my private parts, and very professionally gave me the best massage I have ever had. Daniel, quite simply, was the closest thing to perfect for me that I had ever found. This, at the time, was pretty profound.

Sadly, of course, I had to fly back to Melbourne, and Daniel drove me back to the airport and waited with me till I had to board the plane. We were both quite sad as we were clearly smitten with each other. I remember Daniel walking away from the gate lounge, and looking back at me with an expression on his face I will never forget. He seemed so sad.

Daniel continued to text me for the next few weeks, declaring enormous feelings for me, and how much he was missing me. And I too was returning similar declarations for him. I'd never met anyone like Daniel before and probably never will again. He certainly had set the bar high.

Sometime later, Daniel's texts became less frequent. Used to pretty much his daily texts, I was a little concerned, but not overly. I figured he was particularly busy, at that time. Eventually, there were no more texts. Then finally one day, months later he sent me a long text explaining how he had been very ill and had been in and out of hospitals with an extremely nasty jaw infection. However, in this same text he told me how much I meant to him, and he was so very, very sorry that he'd not been in touch. He would soon be on the mend, and back to his cabin again. Also that I was on his mind constantly.

When I called his mobile number, there was no answer and no voice mail. I figured that he must still be in hospital, where I believed mobile phones to be still pretty much banned, so I simply text him back with my concerns for his health, and to keep me updated. Also, that he meant a lot to me too.

Many, many more weeks passed without a word. I had sent probably 3-4 texts in the meantime to no avail. I figured he had died, or was brain dead or something. None of his family would know about me, so there would be nobody around to let me know.

Then another text from Daniel. He's still crook, and still laid up. But thinks of me often, and so on and so on.

By now, I'm starting to get cranky.

Did he simply use me? And if that's all it was, why would he go on and on, long after with words of love? He surely was a riddle. Even his texts became a riddle to decipher. And why, oh why doesn't he simply pick up his phone and call me? Have they chopped out his tongue?

After much deliberation on my part, I sent Daniel a final text advising him that I simply didn't want to play the games anymore. The riddles were too complex. I thanked him for our amazing time together and wished him well.

I would be lying if I said Daniel didn't hurt me. He is the only man I've ever met who could've broken my heart. He didn't. My heart is not broken, as Daniel didn't let me get close enough for that to happen. But he sure as hell, made me feel good. Then in the end, it was so sad

However, I was brave, I was strong, I was true, I was kind and I sure as hell was grateful.

Chapter 14

Sometime later, I opened my laptop and popped back into the "Lolly Shop" again.

Ricky was another catastrophe waiting to happen. This one was a doozie, and clearly I had lost my brains again.

I met Ricky on RSVP, one of the more respectable online dating sites. His profile was simply amazing. His photos, although were taken over a 10 year time frame, showed a larger than life, confident man with a broad and cheeky smile. He was very tall too, and within my age criteria. However, the biggest attraction of all was he was a musician. I just love the thought of being with someone who can play an instrument, doesn't really matter what instrument, but someone who has a genuine love for music, can always get my interest.

I met Ricky at an outdoor pub not far away from where we both lived, and literally sat there for more than 4 hours listening to this guy talk about the wonderful experiences he had had through his life. He had the art of communication down to a tee.

Ricky had also been a body guard for members of the Rolling Stones, and also claimed his beautiful daughter, who is apparently a stunning model in New York, was the god daughter of Mick Jagger. He even invited me to her upcoming 21st birthday, which was to be held at a secret location in the city somewhere, and Mick Jagger was going to pop in at some stage, and sing to her. I accepted of course. Who wouldn't?

His young and stunningly beautiful Native American wife had sadly died of breast cancer some years earlier, and he was looking for his soul mate.

Ricky claimed he could play the guitar, piano, sax and harp. I remember thinking, what an extraordinary man!

He also wrote music and songs, and he simply had me enthralled with this talent. Some of his work had been recorded by well-known artists. He spoke to the waiters and the people sitting around us in the pub like he was their best buddy, and literally had me in stitches most of the night. He called me "babe" a lot, and reckoned that he and I were the perfect match.

His elderly mother, who was suffering from dementia, lived in Ricky's house in a lovely suburb in Melbourne. He told me how much he loved his mum, and is always there for her, and it's his absolute pleasure to give up a part of his life and career, to take care of her to the best of his ability.

We ate and drank pretty well that night, and he flashed around his credit cards at the end of the evening. He begged me to ride a taxi into the city with him, to kick on some more at one of the nightclubs that he frequented often. I declined, as by then my head was swimming, and came home.

We had arranged to meet again in the next few days. We had a couple more dates, not dissimilar to the first, with me doing most of the listening. This man was wonderful company. He made me laugh so much, and we had a fantastic time together. He phoned or messaged me 2-3 times a day, and just seemed a genuine, sweet and very funny guy.

A couple of weeks later, Ricky invited me to a BBQ at his friend's house. I remember it was one of those stinking, hot, humid Melbourne days, and he had asked if I could pick him up from his home, and drive us both to the BBQ. He gave me his address, but said he would meet me on the corner of his street. I never questioned this ... just picked him up, then off we went.

We somehow became very lost, (not unusual for me), and by the time we arrived, the BBQ was in full swing. There were only probably about 15 people there, but except for the lovely lady, Deb, that was hosting it, the rest were pretty smashed or stoned. There were also a couple of bikers there who I didn't really like the look of at first. Turned out they were actually friendly guys ... it's just that Hells Angels thing that can be a little spooky.

I had brought a couple of bottles of wine with me, assuming that Ricky would be probably drinking beer, which we could pick up on our way. He never mentioned it, so I figured he would share some of my wine. I remember thinking at the time I picked him up, he seemed like he was bursting out of his skin, so full of life and yarns …. The man talked a hell of a lot. It didn't occur to me that he was already half smashed then. Or perhaps off his face on something dodgy

I had just sat down to talk to another lady at this BBQ, when Ricky asked me to drive to the nearby drive in bottle shop, and get him some Coronas and maybe a pack of smokes. I could see he had very quickly got into my wine, and as he was too drunk to drive, I drove to the shop and bought him half a dozen Coronas and a pack of smokes (which aren't exactly cheap anymore).

"Babe", he said when I returned," you are the most beautiful woman in the world, and can you whack some lemon into these for me?" "And while you're up there, grab us a bite will ya?" "Jeez luv, your blood's worth bottling!" … lovely!

Sometime later, Ricky asked me to go back to the bottle shop again, as there was no more beer. I offered him some of my wine, but nope it had to be Coronas. I had had one wine, while I was there and had switched to water, because it was just way too hot to enjoy wine, and I was aware that I was going to be driving home. Also I'm not that rapt in beer.

I did go back to the bottle shop and bought him some more bloody Coronas, against my better judgement, and brought them back to him. At this stage no money had passed hands, but I figured he'd fix me up later. I had pretty much had enough, as I was the only one there still sober, it was getting late and time to head home.

To launch Ricky's bum out of that seat and into my car was exhausting. He simply didn't want to go. So I figured I should just leave him there, but the old good manners kicked in again, and I finally got his arse into my car and incredibly got him home, without getting lost again.

By this stage, Ricky was as full as a state school. He was all slimy, blubbery lips and creepy hands, with smelly breath and words of passion. We arrived at the street where I had picked him up, and I asked him what number he lived in. He told me and I damn near drove him right up the driveway and through the front door. Getting him out of the car was another massive effort, but eventually he hauled himself out of the car. With his unique words of passion, and lots of "babes" thrown in, he clearly wanted to see me again and make amends for his very ordinary behaviour.

I found out the next day, when I phoned Deb, to thank her for the BBQ that Ricky is in fact living with his mum, as he has no money of his own, and is an alcoholic and a junkie. His mum looks after him and has done so for years.

Deb and I are now very good friends, and she is no longer friends with Ricky, as he has lied to her and their friends for years, and although, probably in need of therapy or some sort of help, is still a pain in the bum for many.

He doesn't know Mick Jagger, he never was a body guard, he probably has a daughter somewhere, but we are not sure if she's a model or if she's turning 21, and having a party with a Mick Jagger drop in.... Oh and also, his wife had left him. No kidding?

Nor, to the best of Deb's knowledge did Ricky play any instruments.

At one point in this awful relationship, I was very concerned for my own personal safety.

It was an evening that I had spent with Ricky, who as usual had managed to get himself very intoxicated. By the way, I never saw evidence of Ricky doing any drugs, but it was clear that he was also as high as a kite on something, this particular evening.

Maybe, on some of his frequent visits to the Gents, he was taking something that was very dodgy. I just don't know for sure, but Ricky would be literally jumping out of his skin on some of these outings we had.

As usual, I was doing the driving, so I could only really have one glass of wine, or maybe 2, depending on how long we were out together.

He was begging me to drive us into the city, so that he could continue what was left of the evening with some of his mates. I should come, he said, I would have a blast.

It was very late, and Ricky was sitting in my passenger seat, singing away merrily, and shooting out directions for me, which turned out to be always wrong. We were heading back to his home, where I was going to drop him off, and continue my way home. I had told him a trillion times, I didn't want to go into the city, but he could get a cab if he wanted, but I would take him home on my way. Figured, he could probably work it out from there himself.

Ricky was also an avid fan of the mobile phone. He was forever phoning people, and texting them, before, during, and after dinner, or when we were driving or simply walking around. He loved that bloody thing.

Unless there is some sort of an emergency, and you need to keep your mobile phone handy, I tend not to use it when I'm out. I think it's just rudeness to be sitting with someone, and they are chatting away to someone else.

Anyway, Ricky was at it again, and was clearly trying to organise someone to pick him up and take him out again.

He asked me to pull over about 1 km from his house. I kerbed my car, and waited for Ricky to get out. He was all up for the usual cuddle and kiss thing, but I just wasn't in the mood, and was keen to get him out and on his way.

The next thing I knew, someone had climbed in behind me into the back seat of my car. It was pitch dark, and I couldn't see him. A rather soft and raspy voice said something like "G'day little lady". Ricky clearly knew the guy, as they were doing the old high 5's etc. Shit I was as uncomfortable as all hell.

The fact that this total stranger had just let himself into the back seat of my car, and I couldn't see him at all, was quite confronting. Images of ending up a dismembered, raped and strangled body were rushing through my head.

I told him to get the fuck out of my car.

Language I don't really use normally, but I was scared shitless. In hindsight, this could've been the worst thing to say, as it may have escalated into a possibly very dangerous situation. This guy could've been on meth or anything, and could've become very nasty.

He asked me to be polite, and perhaps share a drink with him. Ricky could see I was dead serious, and I yelled at both of them to get out of my car now, or I will call the police.

What an absolute idiot I was!

Although, they did eventually get out of my car, after me abusing the blazes out of Ricky and this dark shadow in my backseat, for what seemed like ages, I was still shaking all the way home, and furiously gave myself a thorough talking to.

I had allowed myself to get into a very dangerous situation, which could've been catastrophic.

I had always prided myself on being very aware of my surroundings, and personal safety, but in this particular instance, I had thrown that all out the window.

Chapter 15

I have always tried to take people the way I find them. I am so trusting. I reckon I always will be.

Once again, I need to mention, I really couldn't have cared less what Ricky did or who he was.

It doesn't worry me what people might do for a living, where they live, or how much money they make. If people could just be honest from the start, life would be so much easier.

Crikey, it's hard enough to be in your mid-fifties, and on your own, without making things so much harder than they need to be.

Some months later, I noticed Ricky's profile on another dating site, with the same pictures and profile he had when I first saw him, and exactly the same blurb about his music and passion for writing songs etc.

The "Ricky's" of this dating world, although probably need genuine help, are a massive pain in the arse.

They waste your time, although they talk the talk, and walk the walk. Incidentally, I never received that $128.00 he owed me. The bastard.....

Next?

There is a song that most of us know, probably word for word.

It is an Eagles' song called "Desperado". I think it was released in the early 1970's, and was written by Glenn Frey and Don Henley. Another artist of the time was Linda Ronstadt, who also recorded it, and she sang it beautifully. It is a song, which I adore. The lyrics and the tune itself are just wonderful.

There are two lines right at the end of that song that haunt me.

"You better let somebody love you
Before it's tooo oooo ooooooooo late".

There, in those 2 simple lines of that extraordinary song, is a major concern of mine.

Perhaps, I'm just being way too fussy. Why won't I let anyone in?

Also, what the hell do I actually want, exactly?

"The tooo oooo oooooooooo late" lyric scares me to death. Too late, is not where I want to be at all.

I reckon I've given this dating journey a massive effort, particularly in the last 4-5 months. Am also very aware that it's probably about time to give it all a bit of a rest again, and maybe concentrate on something else for a while. Such as my massage business. I have put in very little effort with this, since I qualified. Which is bloody stupid, as I truly worked my arse off to qualify in the first place?

So I guess I'm at another crossroad in life.

We've all been here at some stage or another. It's not such an awful place to get to, as it makes you question your direction, and sometimes, you simply need to back up a little and go left, or go forward a bit and turn right. You hope you will find the right way very soon.

It's not like we can Google it!

For me, it's like having a little being, someone very tiny, sitting on my shoulder, day after day, and particularly night after night, taunting me with words such as "Better get a move on woman, you're not getting any younger here", or "Find yourself a man fast, or you're gonna die well and truly alone".

I will keep searching for my elusive man. My lover. My best friend.
My someone who will talk to me, listen to me, as I will him.
My someone who can share in the little things that mean so much,
Will see all my faults, my imperfections and there are many for sure,
But I will see his too, and want to embrace them,
Then hold on to our dreams and
Walk hand in hand till we can no longer walk
And simply be as one until we are gone.

Wouldn't this be wonderful?
I know he is out there somewhere. It's just a matter of time.

The men I have known, have come and gone
Some have left a mere smudge
Others, a distinct fingerprint
Some even a memorable touch
But, in the case of the Daniels, and the Jerrys of this world
One bloody large and slow to heal bruise.

We, that is the "we" who are now in our fifties, sixties and beyond, had no way of knowing, that one day, we might be left on the proverbial "dung heap" of life.

Our marriages or partnerships have long gone, our children (if we were lucky enough to have them) have moved on, perhaps married with children of their own.

Our security, stability and our sense of worth is shattered. The dreams we had shared and looked so forward to have vanished, and we virtually have to start all over again. It is incredibly difficult. There are days you want to just get off the merry go round, and maybe join a religious sect or a nunnery.

It really doesn't matter if you did the leaving, or you were the one who was left. You have been abandoned either way, in some shape or form, no matter how you look at it. It is bewildering.

The rules have changed a hell of a lot too. Dating now, compared to when you were a young man or woman, is so different. It can all get a little chaotic, and can be just damn confronting.

The Women's Liberation Movement had a massive impact on the women in the 50's, 60's and 70's. I will probably get myself in big trouble with this comment, but I kind of liked things the way they were then. Not all of them, for sure. But there was calmness, and everyone seemed to know the order of things.

Damn it, I still love it when a man opens a car door for me. I love it when they can sometimes take your arm and guide you over the road. Or they might carry your suitcase or bags for you. I'm also pretty sure that there are still many women out there who would agree with me.

Of course, we could've bloody done it ourselves, but really, it was still damn nice they did. I'm not sure if too many men bother with all this now. Why would they?

Although, my early married life had started in the late 70's, there was some structure back then, and we all knew where we stood, and it wasn't difficult. I personally had no problem with it.

Of course many did. Nor do I intend to debate the issue, in this book. It's really not necessary, and these thoughts nowadays are pretty much redundant anyhow.

Life as we knew it back then has changed so much.

Chapter 16

Met a sweet man recently by the name of Simon. Dark hair, quite tall and medium build. He's a Virgo and loves to sail. He has competed two or three times, in the Sydney to Hobart Yacht Race. He owns the yacht and he is the Skipper. Sailing has always been something that I would love to learn one day and it's definitely on my "bucket list". Simon also lives in Whoop Whoop.

We arranged to meet for lunch not far from my home, and chatted away happily for a few hours.

Simon is an amazing story teller. I was lucky enough to listen to him relate his previous attempt in that Sydney to Hobart Yacht Race; complete with a near capsize, and the awesome effort it took for he and his incredibly brave and supportive crew to complete the race.

As he was telling me his story, particularly the part when they had all damn near drowned, he had tears in his eyes. He was referring to the bravery of his crew, but particularly their support when each and every one of them had the choice to bail out of the race, but had chosen to stay on and finish. It was a very moving experience for Simon and the tears in his eyes clearly proved it.

Right there, I knew, I wanted to see this man again.

No, he's not particularly great looking, he's not that tall, nor was I in a state of high excitement, but right there he had my undivided attention. He had showed emotion openly with me, and I'm really a complete stranger.

You don't often get to see that. On a first date, it was quite remarkable. I like that. I like that a lot. So I plan to meet Simon again.

The day after I had dated Simon, I had also arranged to meet another fella named Richard.

Richard is an Aries, tall, with salt and pepper hair, nice build and a wicked smile. We had previously organised to meet over a coffee in the afternoon. Once again, this man lives in Whoop Whoop. So, it was very nice that he had driven so far to meet me.

It has become apparent that there are a lot of men who live in Whoop Whoop. Some of them may find that there are many women out there, just like me, who live in Whoop Whoop too.

You get to do a lot of driving whilst you're dating. I have found parts of Melbourne, I didn't know existed.

Unfortunately, Richard had chosen the venue for our first date, and had clearly buggered it up.

We were literally sitting at a table on the footpath, right near one of the busiest roads in Melbourne.

Our conversation was had in between the comings and goings of every truck, bus, fire engine and motor bike that hurtled past at a great rate, that afternoon. At one stage, an ambulance whistled past complete with siren. There was no indoor seating to be seen, so there we were. The coffee was surprisingly good, and we were there about two hours slightly deaf, but happy.

I like Richard too. He seems very genuine, has a great sense of humour and seems to like me.

So, now I have a couple on the go. Not sure how this is going to work, but the great thing with first time dating, is you can take your time with the second and subsequent dates, and you will hopefully make up your mind soon enough which one you prefer.

It is a "Lolly Shop" after all.

You really like bullets and others like milk bottles! Or you have a passion for those liquorice allsorts, while they may give someone else gas.

There are times of course that you need to be strong enough to handle the inevitable knock backs.

There will be men out there on these dating sites, who are just not interested in you, and hopefully will let you know early in the piece, so you can get on with it. This can be done quickly and neatly on the dating site, and no harm is done.

However, this may occur after the first date. Always a bit harder here, as you have met, and may have thought something with potential was brewing.

It's always a bit difficult to digest if you get a message or text afterwards from that same fella you just met, with the words "Sorry it's just not working for me, but thanks for lunch/or coffee anyway and it was a pleasure to meet you."

However, I sure as hell prefer that, to simply hearing nothing more. No text, message or phone call. You simply never hear from them again. Awful.

This to me, apart from being quite rude, is very cowardly. Later, I always feel that perhaps it was just as well, because that guy clearly wasn't such a great fella anyway. No backbone.

Which reminds me of a date I had, with a very pleasant looking man From the Ballarat area. We had exchanged texts and phone calls over a fortnight or so, and Peter sounded damn near perfect. Tall, fair, well-educated and with a quirky sense of humour. He had kindly acceded to my request to drive down to Melbourne to meet me, and we had arranged to meet not far from my home.

I sat down at the outdoor cafe a little early, and watched him alight from his black BMW, and gracefully make his way over the street towards me.

With the perfunctory kiss on the cheek and lots of big smiles, we sat down and chatted happily away for the next few hours like a house on fire. I then suggested a wander around the parks nearby to stretch our legs and continue our time together. I had brought my little dog, as he's no trouble at all, and I knew he'd love a walk. Peter seemed to really like dogs, which was a huge plus for me.

After our walk, we headed back to the same cafe for a coffee and chatted some more. Now for all intents and purposes, I thought we had sincerely hit it off. This man seemed genuinely interested and very content in my company. He had even shown me photos of his children and his home, which was lovely. I figured that I was on to something here, and wouldn't it all be lovely if it worked.

We finished our date on a seemingly high note, and said our goodbyes.

I never heard from him again.

Chapter 17

Not long after meeting Peter, I met Adam (a Taurus) on line. He's from Whoop Whoop too, and lives an eight and half hour drive from me. Really convenient.

However, Adam is a musician. He totally had my attention. We conversed daily, then swapped email addresses, chatting away happily for a few more weeks.

Adam is very well known in his place of residence as a fine singer, songwriter and an excellent guitarist, and he and a very pretty young woman, Meredith, have a unique sound and a refreshing honesty in their voices that blend together beautifully. The two of them play regularly at various pubs and festivals, in and around the area they live, and have recorded many fine records together.

It was also just lovely to chat to someone who loves music as much as I do.

Adam drove the eight and half hour journey to meet me recently. An amazing effort on his part, but he convinced me that the change of scenery would do him good.

We organised to meet at a cafe not far from where I live, for a late breakfast. A tall, thin man, with short, curly hair. I could've simply chatted to him all day. He has so much depth and soul, but he's switched on and very funny as well. He later played his superb guitar and sang for me, and I was in awe of his talent. It was like I'd simply switched on the radio. That's how good he was.

After a few hours, Adam decided he would drive home. Bloody incredible. Such a long drive for him, but he was keen to get going. He had only been in the state for 24 hours.

Adam and I will probably be friends for ever. He is an absolute sweetheart, and I'm so rapt that I met him. He is someone you would be very lucky to find in your entire life, and I am so grateful I've found him.

I had a text from Simon the Sailor Man, the other day, which had actually touched a nerve with me, on that first date. The one who had shown some pure and open emotion. He feels the distance between us could become a problem, and in his words "he's just not feeling it", and "thankyou for a lovely lunch". I should say here, that it would have been nicer to have had a phone call instead of the text. However, I was pleased he had been upfront with me.

It is just so damn refreshing when people are simply honest and pleasant with each other.

I liked Simon, but it is not the end of the world if he doesn't wish to continue any further.

So much better to be told straight, nice and early so you both can get on with it.

We bare our souls every time we join a dating site. As I have said, it is a very brave thing to do.

It is absolutely necessary and right that we will be knocked back left, right and centre, from time to time.

No matter how cute, clever and compatible you think you may be, not everyone will agree, and will hopefully let you know, fairly soon. It's simply a part of life. The challenge is to pick yourself up, dust yourself off and simply get on with it.

At some point or another, one needs a definite break from online dating.

I always know when that time has come. Time to close down my account and delete the apps from my pc and mobile. I know because I tend to become a bit of a smart arse.

Best to explain this by saying that I simply get to the point of having had enough of the constant necessity to open profiles, responding to each and every kiss and or wink, and the cluttering up in my inbox.

I basically become quite short and rude to other members, and start deleting profiles without really reading them through properly. I begin to only look for someone who I think is good looking, (which is stupid), and worse start talking to people quite carelessly. I know then, it's time for me to give it all away for a while.

You are jaded, and worse you are stale. Time to have a break for sure.

It's no big deal. Even the sites themselves are obviously aware that members will go through this at some stage or another, and allow you to close down your profile, while keeping your account active until you are ready to take it all up again, later down the track. It also keeps the bucks rolling in for them too, but I think it's still a sensible idea. You really don't want to have to start all over again with your profile and photographs.

At this point, it's probably very good manners to advise any current members who you have been chatting to, that you are intending to resign your membership for a while. If there are any who you might want to keep chatting to, and they you, you can get their private emails or mobile numbers, and continue at a later time.

You may be wondering now, that you've come to the end of this little book, why the hell doesn't she simply give it all away? She's clearly had a god-awful time, and she hasn't met ANYONE with whom she could settle down. Why the hell does she keep going? You might also have come to the conclusion that online dating is just too difficult, exhausting and time consuming.

You would be spot on with that.

I know I will keep at it, on again and off again, until I find someone who I want to spend the rest of my life with.

Some people can be at peace with themselves going about their business alone, and feel quite content.

Some women, I know, are more than happy to live the rest of their lives by themselves, and perfectly fine with their own company. They generally have a great network of friends, male and female, and don't really want or need anyone else in their lives. Bloody good luck to them.

They think I'm quite mad, and I reckon they are!

It's just not for me.

So I'll keep putting myself out there, and I will persevere with whatever it takes to find "my man".

I know he's out there somewhere.

I expect he's looking for me, as hard as I'm looking for him.

To all those lovely and lucky people who have met their matches, whether it be a partner, husband, wife, girlfriend, or boyfriend on any of the numerous and diverse dating sites out there:-

Well done, and a huge congratulations to you all!

I have no intention of putting down the actual dating sites themselves. They are there for a very good reason, and I for one would never criticize their intention. Although I'm sure there are a lot of people making heaps of money out of the process. Good luck to them. They came up with a fabulous idea and made it work.

<u>Sociopaths</u>

They walk amongst us every day!

A classic sociopath has charm in bucket loads. They have a "glow" about them, and tend to attract a huge following with their high charisma. They often appear to be sexy or have a strong sexual attraction. Weird fetishes and over-the-top sexual appetites are common. (Clearly in my relationship with Jerry, my pampered feet were his passion).

A sociopath is more intense, and tends towards bizarre and erratic behaviour. Risk taking and irrational behaviour is common. (Jerry's horrendous driving and his threats to jump off the seventeenth floor from our building pretty much fall into this category).

They can simply lie their heads off about anything that they desire to the point of absurdity. However, they are so clever that in the telling of the story it can sound so believable at the time. (Jerry's stories about his stomach cancer, his football achievements, the woman stalker with the scissors and all the other crap that I swallowed hook, line and sinker).

They are delusional and literally believe that what they say becomes truth, merely because they say it.

Also, another classic trait is a need to dominate others and "win" at all costs. They viciously defend these lies and hate to lose any argument. Apologies or remorse are non-existent, as they are never wrong. They cannot feel guilt, and will often go on the attack if necessary. (My passport and bank statements).

They also have an incapacity to feel love. They are very adept at feigning love or compassion, but it's a self-serving love. In other words, it's just to get what they want from you.

They don't actually FEEL love in the way that you and I do.

Extracted from "The Sociopath Next Door". Martha Stout. American Psychologist and Author.

Lightning Source UK Ltd.
Milton Keynes UK
UKOW04f0349120915

258472UK00001B/55/P